Daniel Brande is a prolific writer, consummate marketing practitioner, and eminent award-winning journalist with over 30 years of experience. Blending journalism with marketing, Daniel creates distinctive media products. At the Ghana Broadcasting Corporation and United Nations where he worked for over three decades, his media productions stood out. As a Reuters Fellow at the University of Oxford, Daniel has been a driving force in the media space, freelancing for several international radio stations and magazines with impactful, inventive works. Conveyed in succinct, vivid, lucid language, Daniel's writings and radio productions make an impression on society.

To my late Mom and Dad,

I conceived the idea of writing this book to honor you,

But you were called to your Maker,

Long before I even began the writing process.

The writing is now over,

And here is the book,

It's yours, Mom and Dad,

In memory of your sacrifices and dedication to my upbringing.

Daniel Brande

WHISPERS OF JOY AND MURMURS OF LOVE

AUSTIN MACAULEY PUBLISHERS™
LONDON • CAMBRIDGE • NEW YORK • SHARJAH

Ordering Information
Quantity sales: Special discounts are available on quantity purchases by corporations, associations, and others. For details, contact the publisher at the address below.

Publisher's Cataloging-in-Publication data
Brande, Daniel
Whispers of Joy and Murmurs of Love

ISBN 9798886932140 (Paperback)
ISBN 9798886932157 (ePub e-book)

Library of Congress Control Number: 2023922834

www.austinmacauley.com/us

First Published 2024
Austin Macauley Publishers LLC
40 Wall Street, 33rd Floor, Suite 3302
New York, NY 10005
USA

mail-usa@austinmacauley.com
+1 (646) 5125767

I could not have done it alone. No. There were people who, in diverse ways, propelled me to piece together this narrative. From idea-generation, through research and editing, to cover designing and publishing, I have a long list of people to thank, for investing their time and energies in assisting me to create this book.

My first thanks of appreciation go to God for the gift of life, and the gift of people who helped me scale through an otherwise unassailable terrain to undertake this intellectual expedition.

From the depth of my heart, also pours out special thanks of gratitude to my wife, Gloria; my son, Selasi, and my daughter, Emefa; my siblings, the Azalekors: John, Kweku, Yaw, Willie, and Patrick; not forgetting my son-in-law, Nana Yaw; as well as my sisters-in-law, Becky, Prudence, and Evelyn. They provided the needed encouragement that melted away the gloom and doom that hovered over commitment and success at the various stages of the writing process. I owe them an undying gratitude.

I am highly indebted to Winifred Assan for reviewing the manuscript and offering suggestions to lift the spirit of the book. I am eternally grateful to her.

I also express my heart-felt appreciation to the cover designer and the publishers for expertly clothing the book in its deserved image. I cherish their contribution.

Finally, this list: Dan Afari-Yeboah, Kojo Mensah, Comfort Whitfield, Clement Nkumbe, Kingsford Oppong-Danso, Alex Ofori Karikari, John Abbah, Evelyn Tetteh, Ebenezer Odjawo, Francis Mensah, Alex Ashie; a list of professional colleagues with whom I share a common vision. We always agree and disagree on how to propel this vision. Their wise counseling opened the eyes of my heart to see beyond the ordinary to mold this book in a creative and visionary mode. I am grateful to them all.

Table of Content

Introduction   11

Chapter One: The Miscarriage at the Marketplace   14

Chapter Two: Preparation Toward the Great
Zado Festival   22

Chapter Three: The Zado Festival and the Sinless Girls   28

Chapter Four: Fallouts from the Eventful Zado Festival   37

Chapter Five: Two Beauty Goddesses at Cross-Purposes 45

Chapter Six: The Visit of the Mystery Girl   58

Chapter Seven: The Invitation of the Zale Family to
the King's Palace   68

Chapter Eight: Voberian Emperor in Search of
Regional Peace   81

Chapter Nine: The Ground-Breaking Summit of
Heads of State   91

Chapter Ten: The New-Look Sunrise Hemisphere   108

Chapter Eleven: The Wedding of the Century   122

Introduction

This is a product of the mind's eye. There is no doubt about it. However, it takes you on a lively journey to the reality of the peccable world we live in. On this journey, you will trip over potholes of greed and egoism, slip on landmines of conflict and hegemony, and swim in lovefests of joy and happiness. And finally, you reach your destination, *Whispers of Joy and Murmurs of Love*, on a unique landmass called the Sunrise Hemisphere. On this continent, are seven nations that are immensely homogenous in language but exceedingly diverse in politics. They speak the same language but practice diverging forms of government. Each of the seven states has cultivated its own political ideology, which it stubbornly markets to wield its pride and prejudice. Obediently on duty here, are homegrown concoctions of monarchy, theocracy, autocracy, kleptocracy, democracy, kakistocracy, technocracy, and khakistocracy.

One other unique feature of this region is that, its inhabitants look so alike in appearance, that it is very difficult to identify them by their nationalities. Only by their names, their nationalities can be known, as the names are derived from the names of their countries. Despite the seeming ethnic affinity, a citizen from one state cannot marry a citizen from another state. A piece of centuries-old cultural legislation forbids interstate marriage. This cultural taboo, a heinous crime carrying a penalty of banishment, is religiously observed throughout the continent.

Amazingly, the borders of the states here, are defined by geographical features such as rivers, lakes, lagoons, mountains, and valleys, which are very rich in mineral and hydrocarbon resources. Lamentably, claims to these transboundary geographical features have always been the source of interstate rivalries, tensions, and wars in the region. Consequently, the states in the region do not see eye to eye. The only thing they share in common is their rivalry. Every state here appears to be in perpetual tension.

However, unanticipated love between a crown princess from the most powerful state in the region and a poor handsome young man from a rival state leads to an unprecedented royal marriage, celebrated across all the seven states on the continent. The tensions and rancor once ingrained in the DNA of the region, suddenly disappear, paving the way for the demolition of the physical and psychological barriers separating the states.

The entire continent is now clothed in an unprecedented unity. Trade barriers are lifted and states begin trading among themselves. The taboo on interstate marriage is abolished, and young men and women from different nations across the region are walking down the aisle at an alarming rate. Unparalleled development is taking place everywhere in the region.

All able-bodied men and women are at work, and there is an overabundance of everything in the region:

overproduction of food to eat; superabundance of goods and services to satiate human greed; excess of variety to match all egos; overflow of festivity to quench all social gratifications. The people are excited and are expressing their unity-propelled happiness with whispers of joy and murmurs of love. But for how long will the unity be sustained to keep the people whispering their joy and murmuring their love?

Chapter One
The Miscarriage at
the Marketplace

The sun began to doze. And like a golden medallion in the velvet of the horizon, it glowed and glowed, pouring out eye-pleasing scintillating colors. The moment for swapping roles had once again arrived. And the daylight classily handed over the life-custodian duty to darkness, and charmingly retired to bed. Another complete cycle had ended. But the market continued to animate.

A cacophony of sounds of varying decibels took the market hostage. Hither and thither, pleasure-seekers could be heard roaring and barking, machines screaming and snoring, bells tinkling and jingling, while deal makers could be seen whispering and murmuring. All the familiar sights and sounds representative of a breathing occidental market were obediently on duty. The cacophonous atmosphere was markedly punctuated by unvarying moments of hectic haggling and bargaining. Everybody appeared to be buying or selling.

But I was here neither to buy nor sell. I had an utterly different agenda. And in my effort to accomplish my mission, I carried my shapely slim profile, stuck in an impeccable suit, swinging from one end of the market to the other. Everywhere I went, I could not whet my sentimental appetite. And I roamed and roamed and roamed. I toured the entire market. Nothing tempting to arrest my amorous curiosity!

And I took a mental television of the market as I knew it a few years back, and began unquestionably questioning myself. "But is this a real market day for Zo City?" I marveled as I called to mind the erotic goodies that usually overwhelmed the foremost city of Zoland on market days.

"And where are the lip-smacking, juicy, ripe apples that always lit the market sparkling with pomp and pageantry?" I enquired again and immediately followed up with another mind-blowing question.

Have they all been plucked? I wondered as I got drowned in the monologue, knocking around the market.

I became very worried and then decided to go back home. But I knew exactly what would happen to me if I got home without, at least, a promissory note. I would certainly become a tension-relieving commodity to be traded among peers in the neighborhood. They would hurriedly bundle me up and send me to the social theatre and turn me into an article of comic relief, an Aunty Sally. This dilemma disarmed me from making any further move to go back home.

And so, I continued my tour, devotedly observing every human movement. I saw a group of children on an excursion. They were junior high school students from a nearby town. They looked very green and curious and seemed ecstatic, geared up to discover and conquer anything and everything they stumbled upon.

I also came across a group of young men engaged in politics. They were discussing what they identified as the diminishing political returns of Zoland, which, according to them, had translated into the fast-eroding socio-economic fortunes of their fatherland. Politics is a religion I loyally worship. So, I right away stopped and listened to them with engrossed attention. And they talked and talked, raking and dissecting what they identified as the ugly past of the politics of their world.

They blamed the precarious socio-economic portrait of Zoland on the politics of "winner-takes-all," describing it as an act of political terrorism. They called for the prosecution of all Zolandese politicians for subverting the popular revolution that liberated Zoland from foreign hegemony.

They recalled the political ritual of holding elections every four years in their homeland but wondered why this had failed to bring them economic salvation. One of the young men then began propounding a new-found political ideology, he believed, would heal political wounds, and deliver Zolandese from poverty and misery.

His political homily appeared to have won my heart. He called it *zolandocracy* and defined it as a people-centered democracy that empowers all citizens of a country to fully unlock their God-given talents. While it upholds capitalism to the full, *zolandocracy* frowns on exploitation and tasks the state to fully provide the space the individual needs to become an effective player in the business of capitalism. *Zolandocracy* encourages enterprise and innovation but denounces laziness and self-pity.

After listening to the political sermon for a while, I decided to continue the search for a gem, as neat as a new pin, to emit romantic rays into my famished heart. And as I moved a few meters away, I stumbled upon one, a juicily glittering ornament, fizzing with consummate splendor. And straight away, I felt a sharp vibration in my body, and the climatic condition of my body instantly changed. My social tsunami had come ashore and swallowed up my imagination. I became very confused, with my *attention-meter* falling to almost zilch. I stole a look at her, and her watertight beauty bewildered me. She looked gymnastically tall, with geometrically proportional body statistics to match.

Suddenly, I heard a voice saying: "This is your finest moment, take it." I became baffled, not knowing what to do next. I took another look at her infectious, delicious, and comely beauty: cherry lips, slender waist, almond eyes, and delicate eyebrow. What a paragon of beauty! She appeared as pretty as a field of spring flowers, looking elegantly pristine. In fact, she ought to be barred from public view. Her compelling, unexplored good looks could cause dangerous distractions for every probing eye and even halt a moving vehicle!

And the more I gazed at her, the more confused I became. But I mustered courage and moved closer to her. She discovered my presence and denoted a hearty winsome smile at me. I also responded in body language, using the window on the soul, the eye, to communicate to her. She seemed to have understood my message and drew closer. I also drew closer, clinically examining her engaging body geography.

"Hello, can I help you?" she inquired from me in a polite timbre that sounded very musical in my ears.

"Yes," I instantly replied as I hungrily surveyed the entire circumference of her dazzling beauty.

"What do you want me to do for you?" she trumpeted in an audacious tone that shook the very groundwork of the social goodwill I had over the years built for myself, sending me trembling with apprehension.

"I want you to be my friend," I replied with ease, as I began mustering courage, throwing overboard the timidity and trepidation that had overshadowed me.

"Me to be your friend!" she exclaimed hesitantly, staring at me in an enigmatic posture.

"Who are you, and why do you want me to be your friend?" she demanded, as she continually took me captive with her inviting eyes.

"My name is Zaza," I answered back, paused for a while, and added, "I'm a journalist, an accomplished member of the fourth estate of the realm."

"And do you want to have an interview with me?" she inquired as the dialogue appeared to be gathering momentum.

"No, not an interview at all, but something larger and bigger than an interview," I replied.

"If not an interview, then what does a journalist want from me?" she asked in dismay, shaking her head.

I looked into her face eyeball-to-eyeball and then dropped the bombshell.

"I'm looking for someone with whom I can make a home. And you are the elected one to partner me to do so," I said to her in a wobbly voice.

"To partner you make a home?" she demanded in an inflection of anger and bewilderment.

"Home where?" she asked anxiously, while she watched me with searching eyes.

"Sorry, I'm not yet ripe to buy a share in any home-making business. Please, try your luck elsewhere," she said politely and began moving away.

I followed her obsessively as she sped away. The tantalizing golden luscious apple was out of sight. I could not pluck her. Another opportunity missed. I became confused and worried and decided to retreat my path. And I began the homeward journey indolently, meticulously recounting my encounter with the apple-pie beauty.

"At least she has given me a story to tell," I consoled myself, as I deliberated on the abortive summit with the hard-to-make-out traffic stopper.

Another worry weighing me down was how to repackage the disastrous expedition and sell it to my soulmates as a big success. I had promised to bring home a big catch at the end of the marketplace fishing expedition. Now, here I was, with nothing to exhibit, not even a fingerling!

My worries melted into reflective contemplation like the famous Alexander the Great who had conquered the whole world but found it extremely impossible to conquer his own curiosity. And as I got drenched in the stormy contemplation, an idea came up to devise a narrative, beautifully accessorized with black and white lies to present the star-crossed expedition as a resounding success.

I would tell my friends that I bumped into a bevy of foxy ladies who were so overwhelmed by my spick and span appearance, as well as my gentle and intelligent disposition, that they were all eager to have me as their own. I would add that the greatest problem facing me now was how to choose among the pack of equally stunning, good-looking ladies clamoring for me.

The other aspect of the plan was to look very cheerful. But, this, I was not able to do effectively, tried as I did. I appeared very heavy and dozy, hard to lift my limbs. Though my house was not very far-off from the market, I found it extremely difficult to cover the distance. Sodden in contemplations, I meandered and wandered about as if I had taken a large goblet of *apio*, a strong local gin. I grudgingly pulled myself along the widening pathway. And at last, home, here I was; exhausted and confused.

The news of my arrival went through the neighborhood like a blazing fire. And one by one, my friends began streaming to my house. And they were heavily pregnant with great expectations about my amorous fishing expedition. Was it successful or ill-fated? They all wanted to know. And they bombarded me with a missile of questions.

Then, I began relating my story to them. I initiated it with an age-old oriental proverb, which says, "If you refuse to be straight when you are green, you cannot be made straight when you are dry." Without telling them the import of the proverb, I lifted off the lid on my narrative and started pouring it out. As I gave the account, I was shelled with questions from all directions. Initially, I was nervous, hemming and hawing, finding it extremely difficult to contain the bullet of questions raining on me. Suddenly I gained composure, and convincingly and cogently told my story, painting the ill-starred expedition as a huge success.

Chapter Two
Preparation Toward the
Great Zado Festival

Having won over my friends, I decided to look for something to eat. And after enjoying a plate of *akple*, with okro soup, I retired to bed. But I could not sleep as I kept on pondering over my failure to woo the riveting and ravishing girl.

"At 28, I have no one to call mine and continue to wander in the wilderness of erotic lonesomeness," I repeatedly reminded myself during the seemingly long sleepless night. Then, I remembered the Zado festival, which was just two weeks away. I also remembered the stunning spectacle with which Zado is always celebrated: the parade of mouth-watering pretty girls who invade the festival ground, advertising their contagious beauty. I, as well, remembered the throng of clean and tidy-dressed young men who raid the festival ground to lay ambush for the charming ladies.

"Yes, this is the biggest opportunity for me to find a helpmeet," I perked up myself and began regaining my good spirits. The next thought was a winning formula to put on show on that fateful day. "A new dress, a new pair of shoes, a new haircut, a new pair of goggles, a new everything, and in fact, a new look," I concluded.

And how do I get the resources within a fortnight to effectively rebrand my corporate personality for this immense project? I wondered.

"Convince my sister's husband to finance the project," the first thing that came to mind. "Uncle Zale is a generous man who derives comfort from procuring comfort for others. And he has on many occasions done so for me," I recollected while reassuring myself.

"But I also know Uncle Zale to be a very meticulous person who would always want to ensure that every farthing he spends on you adds value to your personal development," I kept in mind as I fine-tuned the strategy for approaching him.

And here I was, looking very timid and scary before Uncle Zale to make a request for money. I was asking for money, not to buy books or undertake any activity to propel me to the towering echelon of scholarship but to attend an entertainment event. "How do I begin this request? And how will he receive it?" These were the fear-mongering questions overwhelming me. Surprisingly, I initiated the request by just reminding him of the great Zado festival which was only a fortnight away, and he took it up from there, enthusiastically crisscrossing the historical lanes that worked together to give birth to the festival.

"Only two weeks away? And will you be attending?" Uncle Zale asked as he began narrating the historic events that led to the institution of the festival.

"After defeating all our enemy states, and even threatening to wage war against the all-powerful Venomous Empire of Voberia, our public enemy number one, which wanted to obliterate Zoland from the surface of the earth, our forebears instituted the Zado festival. The annual cultural celebration is to honor and pay glowing tribute to the gallant men and women, who paid the ultimate price to defend and preserve the territorial integrity of our beloved kingdom," he recounted with pride.

"This is a cultural carnival every youth of Zoland should attend," he insisted, assuring that there would be a sumptuous menu of Zolandese culture on exhibition. "You have to be there with your friends," he urged me on.

"Yes, Uncle, I will be very pleased to be at the festival, but it appears I haven't made the necessary preparations to attend and participate effectively," I hesitantly disclosed in a doleful voice.

"What does a young man like you need to attend an entertainment event?" he challenged in disbelief. "Is it not a beautiful dress with trend-setting accessories to put you on top of the world before your peers as well as a few bucks for amusement and fooling around?" he proposed.

Advertising his trademark cheesy smile, Uncle Zale told me he would provide the funds I needed to procure whatever I desired to adequately participate in the festival. He further told me to create a to-do list to enable me effectively prepare for the cultural fiesta. Armed with the financial assurance from Uncle Zale, I began taking a mental journey into the two-week-away cultural celebration, traveling around its key signposts, swimming in an ecstasy of adventure, exploring, discovering, and inventing.

The following day, Uncle Zale called me and gave me a budget that was twice what I had anticipated. Heart-warming and spirit-lifting piece of news it was. I became highly elated and found it exceedingly demanding to stumble upon the appropriate idiom in human vocabulary to fittingly express my joy.

Having been financially fertilized, the next task was to look for the appropriate branding mix to positively alter my physical appearance to catapult me to the highest rung of the social ladder among peers in Zoland. "And how do I go about executing this all-important project?" I figured out while the sixty-four-thousand-dollar question took hold of me and emotionally kept me a captive.

Finally, I arrived at the tall list of the powerful tools required for the overhauling exercise: a well-tailored stylish three-piece; a pair of immaculate hand-made Italian shoes; a pair of trendy goggles; a neat, dazzling, variegated tie; and a tidy wavy close-cropped haircut. I also added an intoxicating, sexy, aromatic perfume to the list. I was aware of the alluring influence an intoxicating fragrance could have on the aura of the opposite sex. "The seductive perfume will mysteriously draw me to the charming beautiful ladies," I prevailed upon myself.

I also realized that I had to go through a painstaking psychological rebranding to acquire a can-do spirit to supplement the new physical image I was about to be clothed in. And how do I go about this too? Another mind-boggling conundrum to disentangle!

"I have to fight the spirit of fear, conquer it, and, in fact, fully expunge it from my everyday language," I charged myself as I rolled back the past and visited the fine opportunities 'fear' had snatched from my firm grip.

"It was fear that disarmed me from trailing the fine-looking lady I met at the marketplace a few days ago," I vividly recollected and also called to mind how fear drove me away from having a date with my headmaster's lovely daughter who proposed to me last year.

"Fear has been the juggernaut crushing all fortunes crossing my path," I concluded and decided to seek spiritual help from a powerful prayer warrior in my church.

As the minutes rolled into hours, and the hours into days, the countdown to the festival began zeroing into seconds. I had also gotten set with all the accoutrements required for the rebranding project. My prayer warrior friend had, as well, taken me through a seven-day-prayer-and-fasting deliverance, to exorcise the spirits of fear and timidity that had, for long, taken a deep seat in my whole being.

The eve of the festival arrived, and the dress rehearsal. Two close buddies of mine assisted me to conduct it. All was perfect as planned. I was overflowing with confidence. I knew I had mentally and physically prepared for the great occasion.

"Yes, I will be a hot-selling commodity on the festival ground," I visualized as I played a mental video of my expectations of the cultural bazaar. I visualized a rich cultural carnival displayed in an assortment of traditional dresses, drumming, singing, dancing, and flowing rituals. I also expected an assemblage of people from all stations of life, headlined by a herd of stunningly beautiful girls.

"But there will also be tourists from Europe, the Americas, and other nations across the globe, who will be attired in cute western dresses like me," I assumed and hoped I could be boxed up in this highly intellectual and privileged group and enjoy all the courtesies to be extended to them.

Chapter Three
The Zado Festival and
the Sinless Girls

And at last, the festival day came. Saturday it was; bright and sunny. By seven o'clock in the morning, I was in the company of friends seated at the festival ground. Unsurprisingly, I was impeccably dressed for triumph: fully clad in a trend-setting three-piece suit with a neat dazzling variegated cravat to match, tied in with a pair of immaculate hand-made Italian shoes, and tied up with a well-cropped wavy haircut, harmonized by a pair of trendy goggles, while my entire frame was effervescing with a pricey intoxicating, sexy, aromatic perfume.

Dressed to advantage; dressed to kill; dressed to the teeth. What more? I was, indeed, dressed up to the nines, looking snazzy, nifty, seductive, magnetic, and sleek in full feathers. Immeasurable and simply beyond compare!

I virtually became an object of tourism attraction. And all who set eyes on me had a complimentary comment to pass. They talked about my spotless dress; my slick, voguish shoes; my upscale, groovy goggles; my neat, awe-inspiring haircut; and, in fact, my clean-cut, aristocratic, and graceful look. The bright, fruity fragrance I wore, also stabbed people by the nose and warmly drew them to me.

And as I sat down receiving compliments like homage being paid to a king, I looked very blue-blooded and concluded that today could be a destiny-shaping day for me. Then, I surveyed the entire festival ground and noticed that it had begun overflowing in human numbers. However, I detected that the bigwigs—traditional, religious, and political overlords—of Zoland had not yet arrived. Nonetheless, the drums, in diverse sizes and shapes, were fanatically on duty, sending out sounds of different decibels and melodies.

And the hour came for the arrival of the big wheels. First, were the clergy, attired in long-flowing cassocks and smart vestments, displaying various designs and sizes of clerical collars. The clerics looked hallowed and pious in their holy garbs and appeared to have brought down the saintly heaven to the festival ground as they walked sanctimoniously to their seats.

The top brass of the political decision-makers of Zoland followed. In their delightful traditional and Western dresses, and escorted by their armed vigilantes and aides, they waved to the excited crowd and took their seats. Amazingly, the bitter political foes belonging to diverse ideological leanings, who were always bickering and fighting, seemed to have buried their differences. They were seen heartily advertising amiable smiles, hugging one another, and exchanging pleasantries.

Finally, the turn of the chieftains: the kings, queens, and fetish priests; the guardians of Zoland's rich cultural heritage. And a sudden tidal wave of cultural explosion ushered them onto the festival ground. The muskets fired; the drums beat; the horns blew; the voices reverberated; and in unison, the well-rehearsed feet and hands took stately steps and fluid body movements to announce the arrival of the king and his entourage. And suddenly, the ambience transfigured into a seemingly messy, exceedingly rambling, and uncompromisingly incessant assault on the human sense of hearing, as sounds of varying intensity of drumming, firing, cheering, singing, yelling, and whistling conspired to turn out a jamboree of commotion.

Nonetheless, the presence of the king and his retinue transmuted the festival setting into an exhibition hall of royal paraphernalia. On show were golden crowns, gold-trimmed headpieces, gold-plated footwear, as well as golden rings, necklaces, and bracelets, and all the fetching and prepossessing trappings to decorate a king for an important occasion.

Also conspicuous were a range of beautifully carved traditional stools on which the tsars were imposingly seated. The impressive parade of large colorful umbrellas under which the chiefs sought refuge from the blistering sun, could not escape the prying and gossiping eye. Then, the forest of ceremonial staffs; they were unusual, and of varying ornamentations and symbols, telling the seeming untold story of Zoland and its various clans. Fear-evoking amulets, fly-whisks, and gilded muskets were also in the procession to tighten up the eye-catching spectacle on display.

Clad in a resplendent traditional cloth, and fully arrayed in all-gold regalia, from head to toe, the king was carried in a gorgeous jeweled palanquin. With a fly-whisk in one hand

and a short sword in the other, the tsar of Zoland commandingly gave a rendition of an uncommon, attention-grabbing, traditional dance while the passionate teeming crowd responded with roaring cheers. Accompanying the king were sub-chiefs, who also mesmerized the crowd with their dazzling outfits.

And from nowhere emerged a contingent of amulet-decorated, terrifying-looking fetish priests. Armed with muskets, knives, calabashes, bottles of gin, and a live sheep and cow, they began performing a series of eye-popping rituals. They poured libation, invoking the ancestral spirits, and heartlessly slaughtered the live sheep and cow at the feet of the king, amidst the firing of muskets and throbbing of the deified drums. It was a chilling sight to behold, a moving scene that kept playing on my mind from time to time.

Thereafter, the king, drenched in a glittering sea of gilded regalia, gracefully sat in state and began receiving homage from his subjects. The charisma and majesty that ruled the atmosphere as the obeisances, advertised in various forms of body movement, were paid to the overlord, appeared to have taken the sacred institution of Zolandese chieftain to a new level of sophistication.

Now, the time had come for the eleven clans that sum up the stubborn Zoland Kingdom to showcase their unique cultural identity. This is a keenly contested competition held every year and is one of the unique selling points of the festival. A giant trophy and mouth-watering cash prizes are always at stake, but the utmost prize is the pride that goes with becoming the champions. The contest is, however, restricted to only sinless girls in their teens. During the competition, the clans let loose their most beautiful girls; and many young men in Zoland patronize the event with the hope of fishing out some of the untouched girls to become their future wives.

And will this be the opportunity for me also to fish out one of these unmarked girls as a future wife? I wondered as I glued my eyes to the stage. Clan by clan, the young religious females began mounting the stage to churn out the upshot of the months of preparations they had made. And they came in droves, showcasing the superlatives of the known categories of beauty: divine beauty, dreamy beauty, heart-stopping beauty, traffic-stopping beauty, perfect 10 beauty, easy-on-the-eye beauty, drop-dead beauty, and other stunning versions of dramatic beauty. It was a real, super beauty pageant!

The alluring pure girls were half-nakedly dressed in rich colorful clothes unique to their respective clans and accessorized with dangling heavenly beads around the waist, neck, and arms. They overtly advertised their innocent, firm, pointed breasts which looked so warm, and so responsive to touch. With the luscious hanging coconuts drawing out rapt attention, the inexperienced teen beauty queens mesmerized the gathering with wonderful cultural renditions recounting the histories of their respective clans. They sang, danced, and recited free verses extolling the bravery, hard work, and accomplishments of their clans.

After endearing the crowd to an out-of-the-ordinary exhibition of key ingredients of the beauty brewed in Zoland, the amazing, lovely virgins retired, and converged on a special pavilion erected for them at the festival ground. Here, they would interact among themselves, irrespective of their clans, and also receive compliments from their admirers. And this marquee would soon become a beehive of humanity, where neatly dressed, erotically starving young men would congregate to lie in wait for their future better-halves.

However, access to the pavilion was restricted to only holders of a special highly priced pass, which was, even, oversold. Luckily, my friends and I managed to get hold of the elusive pass. With the pass firmly in hand, the seconds and minutes were just ticking by too leisurely for me to have the rare opportunity to interact with the undisturbed, innocent abecedarians. However, the king of Zoland had to deliver his New Year address to his subjects before the floodgates could be opened for us to intermingle with the blessed virgin Marys.

And a percussion of drums roared, and a sweet musical voice rang out, turning out a multiplicity of appellations of the king, and a well-drilled ensemble of young men and women took to the floor, dishing out an unusual menu of war dances. The high point of the festivities had arrived, and a vuvuzela of horns blared out, boomed out, and blasted out. The stage had now been set for the king to deliver his address. In a departure from previous years, the king would not give his speech in the local language but in English, as the festival had taken on international width and breadth with the presence of several thousands of tourists from across the globe. Now, the monarch and the unexpected laconic speech.

"Fellow Zolandese and friends from far and near, I am delighted to be in your midst once again to honor our gallant men and women, who paid the ultimate price to hold together what we all proudly hail today as the Indomitable Kingdom of Zoland. And we promise to chart a path that will make us live up to the indomitability in our name. We aspire to be unassailable in every field of the human congregation, and we will not be complacent. We will strive to better what we see today as the best because the frontiers of human illumination are fast changing. We will go all-out to better the best and make the summit our home in every area of human enterprise.

"As we celebrate this unique occasion, recollecting the gallant deeds of our forebears, we should peep into the future with hope and confidence. We should rededicate ourselves to be responsible citizens, loyally performing our duties, and tenaciously demanding our rights. We should promise to practice politics devoid of corruption, hate, and discrimination. Above all, we should promise to be determined citizens, ready to explore and innovate, to bring refinement to society. If we all agree to travel on the road of excellence, we will continue to excel and be the envy of all the states in the region. And they will continue to wage physical and psychological wars against us in an attempt to derail our forward march.

"However, peaceful as we are, we are always sending them an olive branch to join us build peace for humanity. It is for this reason that we have opened up diplomatic missions in most of our neighboring states, nations that once waged war against us. Fellow Zolandese, I am using this occasion to extend warm regards to the Venomous Empire of Voberia, our archenemy, and express our greatest desire to establish diplomatic relations with them at the ambassadorial level. We are patiently waiting for a word from them.

"Fellow Citizens, Ladies, and Gentlemen, I am sure you were all moved by the wonderful cultural performance displayed by our young girls. Yes, we owe it a duty to preserve our cultural heritage. What you have just witnessed here is only an inkling of the wide array of eye-catching and imagination-arresting sights and sounds Zoland has on sale for curiosity-seekers. Our forests and water bodies are teeming with fascinating animals and fishes, while our skies are lit with an orchestra of birds, eulogizing the creator with awe-inspiring hymns. And our beautiful palm-flanked beaches are waving and beckoning pleasure-seekers for a hug. So, we invite you all, from far and near, to come to Zoland and sample our colorful and hospitable culture. You will not regret it.

"Now, as the commander-in-chief of the Indomitable Armed Forces of Zoland, I wish to assure you all that our security is in good health, and so is our economy. We are indomitable, and we will continue to be unassailable. Thank you all, and God bless the fatherland."

The Zoland overlord's speech was greeted with a standing ovation, submerged in an ear-piercing throbbing of drums and horns. Majestically, he was ushered back to his seat by a retinue of praise singers. Thereafter, the greenlight came for the public to visit the pavilion and interact with the young beauty queens.

And as soon as the announcement was made, a stream of well-dressed young men began flowing to the pavilion. I joined them together with my friends, and suddenly we found ourselves in the holy convent of the Madonnas. They appeared raw, stainless, naive, pristine, virtuous, heavenly, and glorious and looked extremely beautiful and radiantly pleasing to the eye. Their delicate, sublime, bewitching beauty seemed to have worked together with their purity and righteousness to create a magnetic aura around them. Numbering over one hundred, each one of them had a unique hallmark of beauty to arrest the eye and detain the mind in the prison walls of contemplation.

Yes, I was virtually reduced to a prisoner of thoughts, finding it extremely difficult to put thoughts together, to decide on, which of the equally striking beauties to talk to. Finally, my faultless appearance seemed to have bewitched one of them, who beckoned me to her side. And straight away, we began chitchatting. She was really one-of-a-kind: teasingly captivating, temptingly sparkling, provokingly transcendent, and invitingly symmetrical in body statistics. I shook her hand and congratulated her on the splendid performance put up by her clan. She gazed at me and told me she liked my exotic, fashionable, shipshape look, and then asked for my name. We exchanged names and phone numbers. Our heart-to-heart went on and on and traveled beyond the frontiers of formal introduction to a romantic territory.

"I have truly come across her now," I said to myself, as I stared at her once more, bade her goodbye, and waved. She waved back with an appreciative, blissful smile, and said, "We will soon meet and continue from where we left."

Chapter Four
Fallouts from the Eventful
Zado Festival

Having satisfied myself with the effective manner I accomplished the mission that brought me to the festival, I decided to go back home in the company of friends. And as we began leaving the venue, I heard a voice calling "Zaza, Zaza." I turned back, and lo and behold, here she was, the master traffic-stopper, the super beauty queen I met at the market a few weeks ago, whose hard-to-pin-down disposition nearly gave me a heart attack.

"I have been looking for you, all this long; where have you been?" she asked as she firmly held my hand. She denoted a hearty smile, publicizing seductive, delicious, dancing dimples, and told me she had traveled a long distance to the festival, solely to look for me.

"Oh, you look very gorgeous in your dress; I like every component of your look: your suit, your tie, your goggles, your shoes, your haircut, and even your fragrance; all wonderfully blend to make you graceful and delightful to every penetrating eye," she noted, as she increased the intensity of her grip on my hand, while her escort of heavily-built attractive ladies looked on watchfully.

"Do you know that I have been looking for you since we met at the market a few weeks ago?" She unflinchingly confessed and revealed that I was an unfinished story she had been telling her friends and that she urgently needed me to complete the story.

"At the market the other day, you hypnotized me with your glossy look, but today you have taken me a prisoner with your A1 appearance," she conceded.

I could not believe myself; I was confused and short of words. I could not even ask for her name. The only words that came out of my mouth were, "Thank you for the compliments; I am grateful." As she released her hand from mine, she handed over a fat envelope to me, asked for my phone number, and said, "I will call you." And off, she left in the company of her lieutenants, while I intently watched them race away.

My friends, who witnessed the scene, were surprised and began asking me questions. They wanted to know where I knew her, and why she was escorted by ten stoutly-built ladies. My friends were also anxious to know the content of the fat envelope she had given me. Their concerns were many, but I refused to respond to any of them.

As we continued the home-bound journey, I reflected on the eventful encounters: the lively interaction with the charming virgin; and the spur-of-the-moment reunion with the beauty goddess. All this, in my estimation, summed up a successful adventure at the cultural bazaar. I also pondered over the fat envelope, wondering what its content might be. I became very confused with joy, not knowing which of the godsends to celebrate.

Should I celebrate the apparent grabbing of the yummy virgin or the capture of the marvelous beauty empress? And how do I tell Uncle Zale about my encounters with the two ladies? What's more, the fat envelope; should I give it to Uncle Zale to open? These dilemmas weighed me down and kept me chewing over my apparent discovery of a cloudland at the festival ground. I pondered over this until I got home, utterly sodden in rumination.

At home was Uncle Zale, impatiently waiting for me to give him the highlights of the celebrations. And when he saw me in the splendid appearance, he seemed to have been taken aback. And in a low tone, he said, "You look very elegant," and then began asking questions.

"Did you enjoy the festival?" That was the icebreaker, and the questions flowed and flowed, probing every aspect of the cultural get-together. And I took him captive, confidently providing the answers, explaining them in detail, sometimes embellishing them with little white lies laced with a barrel of laughs. However, I did not tell him about my encounters with the two beauty icons, nor did I say anything about the fat envelope in my possession.

"You see how the festival has turned you into an expert in Zolandese culture," he observed after listening to my blow-by-blow narrative of the observance. Then and there, he called my sister to come and admire my well-ordered appearance. Sister Zizi was so impressed with my apple-pier order air that she offered to give me money to buy another classy suit. "Oh yea, that's Zaza my brother conquering the entire Zolandese kingdom," she bragged and reminded me of my childhood dream of becoming a trailblazer in the kingdom. "And I know you are seriously working toward achieving that," she reassured herself, while spurring me on.

After showering, and taking my evening meal, I retired to bed. However, as I was about to sack-out, I was inundated with calls from peers congratulating me on my exploits at the festival. Some, even, trooped to my house to get first-hand information on the purported heroic acts I put up at the festival. However, I refused to disclose what really transpired at the festival. I only told them the event was a big success, and hurriedly saw them off and went back to bed.

And as I was about to nod off in the wee hours, I had a phone call. I initially refused to answer it, knowing it might be one of my numerous small-talk-excited friends, but it continued ringing intermittently until I picked it up. And guess who it was? The unscratched, un-plucked mouth-watering, juicy apple I stumbled upon at the festival, the teen virgin. And in an easy-on-the-ear voice, she said, "Hello, Zaza, I am calling just to express my gratitude to you for lifting me up to the top of the moon today, thank you. We'll be in touch, good night," and then hung up. The good tidings in the brief call lulled me into a deep sleep.

I got up the following morning with an overhang of the experience I had the previous day, dazed with joy and shock. I could not imagine how I was able to successfully dribble my way through the barriers of fear and stiff competition to enjoy enthralling and haunting encounters with the two amazing ladies. In spite of this, I was determined to see the content of the obese envelope in my possession. Having now been "born again," after a seven-day-prayer-and-fasting deliverance, I piously knelt down, said a brief prayer, then opened the envelope. Unbelievably, here was a bundle of 100-US-dollar spanking new banknotes accompanying a one-page letter.

I became very confused, not knowing what to do next. Should I read the letter first or count the money first, a tough call to make. And after mulling over it for a while, I decided to count the money first. And nervously, I began the banknotes' census. One by one, and steadily, the census was over. A hundred pieces in all, amounting to US$10,000. A whopping sum indeed! I had never counted such a huge sum of money in my life. And with an exchange rate of one US dollar to 1,000 Zolandese Zoki, I had already become a millionaire.

This realization made me become more and more confused. "Is the money really mine or is it intended for someone else using me as a go-between?" I mentally covered this tantalizing and meandering lane of contemplation for some time and then decided to read the seemingly mystifying letter, which bore no address and no sender's name.

'Dear husband-in-waiting,

This is mine; and I hope yours is on the way. Mine is to make a bold statement that you are mine, and nothing can snatch you away from me. I don't know what yours contains, but I believe it will be on the same wavelength with mine. The very moment I met you at the market, I knew you would be the greatest thing to happen to my life. And I kept it close to my chest.

It was fear and timidity that unarmed me and prevented me from drawing closer to you. And I regretted it. When I got home, I narrated the missed opportunity to close friends, and we were all sad. However, we resolved to do everything to locate you and own you. No matter the cost of the owning process, we are ever prepared for it. To us, this is a life-or-death mission; and there is nothing under the tongue of man to dissuade us from pursuing and accomplishing it.

I know you will be wondering why I am so desperate to possess you. And this is the why. Many stately and princely young men have crossed my path, but none has so mesmerized and so won my heart than you. Ours seems to be a convergence of comparable chemistries. Not only that. Your persona appears to radiate an aura that is so magnetic that it can even pull down the galaxies in the saintly heaven to our sinful terrestrial orb.

So soon, your charm is dragging me to an irresistible dreamland. And you too, do you find any Shangri-La in me? Yours is beyond bounds: it burns the heart; it haunts the mind; it queries imagination; it generates suspense. And for now, I am keeping you in suspense by not revealing my identity and address. But very soon, this will change. We will know ourselves thoroughly; trading ideas, swapping gifts, and exchanging visits. Until then, I wish you all the best. Take care, and remember that the first step of the tortuous journey to our wedlock has just got underway, and you have to begin adjusting yourself to live up to your new designation, "Husband-in-Waiting."

I read the letter over and over until I meticulously comprehended the import of every word and punctuation mark in it. Then, I conjured up my student days in a literature class and summarized the whole letter in just two phrases: falling for me and hitting the jackpot.

"The Mona Lisa is mine for the taking; she has overtly fallen for me," I declared as I recalled the spirit-lifting and hope-nourishing messages in the letter. I was also excited about the $10,000 cash enclosed in the letter, seeing it as a jackpot that had brought me to the fore of a millionaire, perhaps, the youngest millionaire in the Indomitable Kingdom of Zoland. I became extremely happy.

However, beneath the good news were lingering concerns. First, the realness of the beauty idol I was dealing with. "Is she a human being or a ghost?" This recurring question had reduced me to a miserable soul, strangulating under a heavyweight of meditative thoughts. My other concern was the management of the entire marriage proposal. "I never offered a project management course at school, and how would I manage this huge project trimmed with mouth-watering cash souvenirs and heavily policed by threats and an ever-present contingent of amazons?" This was another heavy load hanging on my neck. "Should I handle it alone or seek the advice of my sister and her husband?" Here too, indecision was the only option available.

These nerve-racking worries completely doused away the rare barbecue of joys and excitements I had harvested at the festival and jealously hoarding. However, I held the perceived quandary secret to myself. I refused to divulge any information on the seeming mystery girl and her mystery letter zipped up with an unbelievable cash gift to anyone. Not even my trusted friends, nor my sister or her husband.

Chapter Five
Two Beauty Goddesses at Cross-Purposes

While consumed by the cash gift and the expressive love letter from the mystery girl, I was, as well, exchanging regular phone calls with Zifi, the beautiful Zolandese virgin I interacted with at the festival. I had even mentioned her to Sister Zizi and Uncle Zale. They were both excited and had asked me to invite her home, promising to give her a stamped-on-your-memory treat. Zifi wholeheartedly accepted the invitation. However, on the eve of the visit, I received a call from the mystery girl, requesting me to meet her at a popular spot, very close to our house on the very day and at the very hour of Zifi's scheduled visit. The new development bogged me down in a quagmire.

"Should I call Zifi and cancel the visit? And how will I explain this to Sister Zizi and Uncle Zale, who had heavily invested in the planned visit? Should I rather not honor the appointment with the mystery girl?" A dichotomous dilemma indeed!

However, as I was obsessively contemplating the either-or dilemma, I heard a knock on my door. It was Uncle Zale, beaming in his customary cheesy smile. He instructed me to call Zifi and inform her to reschedule her visit to the following week. "Your sister and I will be out of town tomorrow," he briefly added and left.

Hurriedly, I relayed the message to Zifi and began preparing for the date with the mystery girl. I decided not to appear gorgeous before her but to just look cute and tidy. I also decided not to be in the company of any friend but to be as solitary as an oyster. The appointed day came, and, at the appointed time, I found myself seated at the appointed spot, beautifully clad in blue jeans with a blue lacrosse T-shirt to match. And of course, I did not forget to wear a suggestive, aromatic fragrance. And after five minutes, there, she emerged, the succulent beauty pin-up, with her usual retinue of bodyguards. She embraced me, and we sat nose to nose, while her bodyguards sat afar, watching us alertly.

And we began the one-to-one. We took a long journey into the future, exploring our vision and mission statements, excessively discussing how we could change the present world of our parents, which we perceived to be contaminated with intolerance, hate, and self-centeredness. However, we did not mention the names of our parents or their hometowns nor did we talk about our own places of birth. As the heart-to-heart got to a crescendo, we began sipping coca cola. And with her eyes directly fixed on mine, I asked her her name and expressed my heartfelt gratitude to her for her innovatory letter and the sweet language in which the contents were poetically conveyed. Furthermore, I thanked her for the unimaginable whopping cash gift she poured on me and prompted her to disclose the source of the money. She just smiled and said, "You will know my name, and where I got the money, as our friendship grows."

After an exhaustive tête-à-tête, lasting over two hours, we decided to call it a day. However, before we parted company, all her ten aides came around to pay me homage. Each had a warm handshake with me, after which their chieftain romantically embraced me and presented me with a beautifully decorated parcel saying, "This is for you; remember me in your sweet dreams." Bursting with an irrepressible emotion, I received the parcel, thanked her, and asked, "When am I seeing you again?" In a tender voice, she replied, "Very soon," and off she went in the company of her aides.

Another unforgettable rendezvous. It warmed the cockles of my heart and brought me heart-felt pleasure. I enjoyed every bit of it. Certainly, I was on cloud nine, delightfully swimming in joyous joy. Like a baby discovering a toy, I repeatedly massaged the parcel in my possession in an attempt to guess its content. However, the more I massaged it, the more confused I became conjecturing its content. I, therefore, decided to abandon the parcel-undressing project and go back home.

Sister Zizi and her husband had returned from their countryside trip before I got home, but I managed to smuggle the parcel into my room without anyone of them seeing it. I locked it up in the same drawer I kept the letter and the $10,000 cash. I vowed not to disclose any information about the mystery girl and her gifts to anyone. I decided to place a total embargo on everything relating to her until she communicated with me again. The decision to provisionally erase her from memory was to enable me psychologically prepare for the just-around-the-corner visit of Zifi.

The rescheduled day for Zifi's visit finally arrived. We adequately prepared for it and were eager to meet her. Drinks of diverse tastes were stocked, and a variety of cuisines were prepared. The hall to host Zifi was beautifully decorated with captivating, color-coordinated flowers. Additionally, it was aromatically perfumed, and musically tuned, emitting a sweet scent and calming, symphonic tunes, thus creating a Christmassy atmosphere. I wore one of my best dresses, looking spotless, while my sister and her husband were smartly dressed. And a few minutes later, Zifi turned up. She was alone, even though she had indicated she would be coming with her two sisters.

She appeared in an up-to-the-minute dazzling outfit, with her profile radiating extreme good looks and incredible charm, giving a breath-taking panoramic view of her out-and-out beauty. She politely greeted Sister Zizi and her husband and tenderly hugged me. I ushered her to her seat and sat beside her, while Sister Zizi and the husband sat together, facing us. I introduced her to my sister and her husband, and the lively conversation began. And after a few minutes, all was over; Zifi was not a stranger. My sister discovered her to be her classmate's sister, while Uncle Zale found out that Zifi was the daughter of his favorite university lecturer. Zifi had come home; and she was aptly at home with us all throughout the extensive, twisty conversation that ushered us into lunch.

And after the toothsome feast, featuring a range of tasty meals, Uncle Zale and Sister Zizi slipped out, leaving us in a blissful lonesomeness. Lonely, we talked and talked, discussing all manner of issues, laughing and giggling as if we had known each other for years. After spending well over four hours with me, Zifi decided to leave. However, before heading off, she went to Uncle Zale and Sister Zizi and thanked them for the warm reception given to her and promised to pay regular visits. Sister Zizi handed over a white envelope to her and instructed me to take her home in Uncle Zale's car, an order I faithfully carried out.

Since then, Zifi had been part and parcel of me, and the entire family, visiting regularly and assisting in the household chores. She always set our home lighting with her infectious smile and her workaholic disposition. Her presence had, for all time, been a festival to celebrate. My sister and the husband had developed a special love for her, repeatedly throwing all sorts of gifts at her. They had even put together a secret plan to make her my helpmate. It appeared Zifi was aware of the plan and was nicodemously working toward its execution.

The love between me and Zifi was deepening to a point of no return. Zifi began occupying almost every space in my heart. However, while this was happening, the mystery girl resurfaced and clandestinely found residence, as a squatter, in the tiny space left in my heart. In fact, she was assiduously working toward having a permanent and lawful residence in my heart. She was making repeated phone calls, floating appetizing sentimental schemes. This inextricable state of affairs created irreconcilable circumstances for me, compelling me to seek refuge in shifting allegiance between the two beauty icons.

However, the advances of the mystery girl were becoming too much to bear. She was calling at ungodly hours and making unimaginable hope-fostering promises laced with fear-mongering jokes. Consequently, I decided to seek expert advice to enable me to make out the real motive behind her plan. But before taking that line of action, I decided to un-wrap the beautiful parcel I received from her a few months ago. And when the wrappings were removed, a whole world of high-priced bits and pieces emerged: a glittering gold watch; a pair of trendy goggles; a pricey perfume; a pair of costly Italian leather shoes; an expensive fashionable leather belt; an ultra-modern camera; and the latest smartphone in town.

There was also a short note posted on a piece of aromatically perfumed white paper bearing the inscription, '*Your heart is my home. Will I also have a home in your heart?*' After reading the heart-gladdening message, I said to myself, "She has done it again," as I vividly summoned up the bulky envelope containing US$10,000, she presented to me a few months ago.

Utterly confused, with no idea of what to do next, I walked straight to Sister Zizi and told her every detail of my adventures with the mystery girl. I began with the star-crossed summit I had with her at the market. I talked about the unscheduled reunion we had at the festival ground, as well as the unbelievably expensive gifts she had sprayed on me, including US$10,000 cash romantically wrapped in a ground-breaking love letter. I also mentioned the recurring phone calls she had been making to me, promising heaven and earth to seal a matrimonial bond with me. I did not forget to tell my sister about the ten stoutly-built beautiful ladies who always accompanied her to her meetings with me.

"What is her name, and where does she come from?" Sister Zizi inquired.

"I don't know her name and where she comes from," I stuttered in a low tone while Sister Zizi stared at me.

"But why didn't you ask for her name? Haven't you been dealing with her for some time now?" Sister Zizi demanded as she continued her probe.

"Yes, I have been dealing with her for well over six months," I told my sister and confided in her that it was me who initiated the matchmaking.

"I met her at the marketplace and proposed to her, and she snobbishly ignored me. I, then, forgot about her entirely, but she re-emerged to stake an undying claim to my heart," I explained.

"Oh, Zaza, and so it was you, who began this whole game; you must know the rules of engagement of the game of love, and play to the rules," Sister Zizi scolded me and questioned why I didn't know her name by now.

"I asked her to tell me her name, but she refused to do so and only said I would know her name as our love grows," I lamented to my sister.

"And the love hasn't grown yet? Is it still at the incubation stage?" Sister Zizi interjected.

"I don't know," I replied and hurriedly took my sister to my room, and opened my can of worms to her. And glittering before her unbelieving eyes were the US$10,000 cash and the expensive gifts as well as the incredible love letter and the well-perfumed romantic note.

My sister began examining them one by one. First, the cash gift. She nervously counted the bundle of the US dollar banknotes and confirmed it to be US$10,000. Then, she examined the pricey gifts, inspecting them one by one. Finally, she read the breath-taking love letter and the brief sentimental note.

Looking confused and speechless, Sister Zizi gazed at me for a while, and asked, "Are you sure you are not dealing with a ghost?"

"I can't tell if she is a ghost or not," I answered, but added a caveat, "however, I cannot understand why she is refusing to disclose her identity; she will not tell me her name, let alone, where she comes from."

As I was speaking to my sister, I began shivering like someone from the tropics exposed to an extremely freezing wintery environment. Realizing that fear had gripped me, my sister held my hand and told me not to be scared, promising to discuss the matter with her husband. She assured me that the so-called mystery girl would soon cease to be a mystery.

Unexpectedly, Sister Zizi shifted her attention from the 'fear virus' that had infected me to the hoard of gifts I had amassed. She picked the sparkling bundle of US dollar banknotes and bragged, "Hey, brother, you are now a millionaire in Zoland, the youngest millionaire, I presume."

I laughed and conceded that I was now a member of the exclusive club of 'wealth of millionaires' in Zoland. Thereafter, I began espousing the massive beauty of the mystery girl, painting a graphic portrayal of every segment of her inimitable beauty: her intoxicating smile that loiters and hypnotizes the heart; the cherry lips, the slender waist, the almond eyes, the dancing dimples, the delicate eyebrow, as well as the well-proportioned body statistics; all tenderly complement to glitteringly install the uniqueness of her beauty. I did not end there. I also extolled her radiogenic voice and the courteous manner she deploys it to gracefully communicate. All these illuminate the graciousness of her inner beauty.

My sister listened to me with rapt attention as I colorfully painted the visual rendering of her sister-in-law-in-waiting and asked, "And so, Zaza, where are you putting beautiful Zifi, if the mystery girl eventually mystifies you into marriage?"

"Oh, that bridge, I will know how to cross it when I get there," I philosophically answered.

Sister Zizi looked at me, laughed, and said, "Men are always men; wherever you find them, they speak the same language."

"Oh, sister, which language; what is that language?" I retorted.

"You know the language; you speak it fluently. Every man on this blue planet speaks this language. It is the language of deceit. And this is the exact language you are trying to speak to the two pretty girlfriends of yours," Sister Zizi pointed out.

"I don't know any language called 'deceit' spoken by all men in the universe," I challenged my sister, reminding her of our parents' unquenchable appetite for iron discipline that had instilled in us sterling virtues with which we conduct our daily affairs.

"Moreover, I have not made any commitment to any of the two ladies," I stated and explained that it was rather the ladies who had been making incredible commitments to me, pledging everything under the sun, even their lives.

My sister responded in laughter and teasingly called me a "Ladies' Man," and immediately left.

From my room, Sister Zizi straightaway went to her husband and gave a vivid account of my adventures with the apparent mystery girl. Thereafter, both rushed to my room and constituted themselves into a court of law, with Uncle Zale assuming the role of a judge, while Sister Zizi doubled as a prosecutor and a counselor.

They subjected me to a severe cross-examination, and asked me to display what they deemed to be court exhibits: the US$10,000 cash gift, the expensive gifts, the love letter, and the sentimental note. They carefully scrutinized the items, after which Uncle Zale gave his verdict. It was a one-sentence judgment: "This is a girl who has wholly given her heart to you; go for it." After pronouncing the "not guilty" verdict, Uncle Zale told me to invite my mystery girl home for lunch.

"I can't get in touch with her, because I don't have her phone number; she always calls me with an unknown number," I explained in an emotion-tinged voice.

"So, everything about your mystery girl is a mystery," Uncle Zale observed in laughter and added, "Anytime she calls, invite her home." And as Uncle Zale was talking to me, my phone rang. I picked up the call, and as divine providence would have it, the mystery girl was on the line. I hurriedly switched on the speaker of the phone for Uncle Zale and Sister Zizi to listen in and discover the angelic voice of their sister-in-law-in-waiting.

Mystery Girl: "Hello, Zaza, how are you? It's been a long time, more than a century for me.

Zaza: "I am fine, my dear. Yes, it's been a long time indeed; and why the long hibernation?"

Mystery Girl: "Oh, Zaza, the perceived long absence was intended just to assess the depth of the love I have for you."

Zaza: "And after the assessment, how deep is it?"

Mystery Girl: "Oh, it's extremely deep; as deep as the void above; as deep as humanity; and as tender as the blue of a baby's eye."

Zaza: "Oh what can I say again? Nothing! You've given all to me, and I have taken all from you. And do you know the depth of my love for you too?

Mystery Girl: "No, I don't know, tell me, Zaza."

Zaza: "I won't tell you now; at the right time and at the right place, you will know it."

Mystery Girl: "I believe so. At the right time and the right place, you will surely demonstrate the depth of the love you have for me."

Zaza: "Oh yes, I will. But there is one thing about you that I find very hard to explain: your generosity; it's beyond human comprehension. And I don't know how to thank you for the wonderful gifts you've poured into me since we met. I have shown them to my sister and her husband, and they were very much touched, and very grateful to you. They've even asked me to invite you home for lunch."

Mystery Girl: "Inviting me home for lunch? That's a great honor. Please, Zaza, tell Uncle Zale and Sister Zizi that I will certainly honor the invitation. They should expect me at their home next Saturday around 12:30 pm. I will be there with friends."

Zaza: "And where do I meet you to bring you home?"

Mystery Girl: "Oh don't worry, Zaza, when I get to Zo City, I will know how to get to Uncle Zale's house. Goodbye, Zaza; best regards to Uncle Zale and Sister Zizi. Take care, and let me always appear in your sweet dreams," she concluded and hung up.

Stone silence descended on us all. Uncle Zale and Sister Zizi were rendered speechless by what they had heard. They were not only surprised by the flowering romantic language in which the entire phone conversation was conducted but were extremely shocked by the fact that the mystery girl knew their names and could pronounce them well.

"Have you ever mentioned our names to your mystery girl?" Uncle Zale broke the long silence with that leading question.

"No," I replied, insisting that I had never mentioned their names to her. "I was also very surprised to hear her mentioning your names," I maintained.

"Then, how was she able to mention my name and that of your sister?" Uncle Zale fired back as he continued subjecting me to a gunshot of questions.

"Please, uncle, I was also surprised by the ease with which she correctly pronounced your names," I affirmed.

"She must indeed, be a mystery girl," Sister Zizi cut in and predicted, "more mysteries await us when she comes here on Saturday."

After the back-and-forth Q&A, we shifted our attention from attempting to unlock the secrecies engulfing the mystery girl to discussing the program we would put up to give her, and her entourage, a rousing, and lingering reception.

"So, she will be coming with friends as she indicated in the phone conversation with you," Uncle Zale inquired.

"Certainly so, Uncle," I confirmed without hesitation.

"And do you know the number of friends that will be accompanying her?" Uncle Zale asked, as he picked a pen and a piece of paper from my table and began scribing down what seemed to be the coefficient of the budget for the lunch.

"I don't know the exact number that will be following her on Saturday; maybe ten, as I always see her moving with ten stoutly-built beautiful ladies," I suggested.

"Oh, it will then, be an episode of the 'Mystery Girl and Her Ten Gladiators' on Saturday," Uncle Zale jokingly said, and we all burst into laughter. We talked about the menu to be served but left it for Sister Zizi to decide.

We were further concerned about Zifi; how to prevent her from gate-crashing the impending get-together. Zifi had virtually become a member of our family and easily popped in without prior notice. Uncle Zale cleverly put together a wonderful program that would ensure that Zifi was away on an equally merry-making mission while the lunch was taking place.

Chapter Six
The Visit of the Mystery Girl

Early on the day of the visit, Uncle Zale and Sister Zizi ensured that everything was well arranged. The banqueting room was beautifully decorated and sweetly fragranced. The ingredients for the yummy menu were finely chopped and adequately massaged for instant conversion into edibility. The assortments of drinks were artistically arranged to whet the agreeable ladylike appetite.

By 11:30 in the morning, we were all elegantly dressed, eagerly waiting for the arrival of the mystery girl. And at exactly midday, she arrived in the company of the ten gladiators. They were gorgeously attired, looking pristinely succulent, with the mystery girl superlatively soaring above the pack in almost every department of prettiness, making her larger than life.

And as she cast her fetching eyes on me, she instantly embraced me and gave me a tight, everlasting hug that communicated deep joy into my heart. Unquestionably, the hug transmitted currents of overpowering bliss across my entire body. I relished every single piece of it. I was indeed, in a transport of delight, feeling extremely happy like a dog with two tails. After briefly shepherding me into the sentimental dreamland, she turned her attention to Sister Zizi and Uncle Zale. She warmly greeted them and surprisingly asked about the whereabouts of their three-year-old son.

"And where is little Zito?" She inquired, as she showcased an excessively gracious smile springing from a seeming flamboyant visage.

"Oh, Zito is playing outside. He will soon join us," Sister Zizi answered in amazement, wondering how the mystery girl could know the name of her son. And as the two were exchanging pleasantries, the mystery girl spotted the boy and said, "Hey, Zito, come here," and the boy ran to her. We were all astonished as the mystery girl held Zito's hand and handed over an assortment of candies to him. The little boy received the gift with a chubby smile from which resounded the complimentary "Thank You" anthem he had been rehearsing with his parents since the first day he ran into a benefactor.

Sister Zizi stole a staggered look at me and the husband, swiftly shifted her attention to the mystery girl, and gleefully ushered her and her train to the banqueting room. And we all followed and took our seats. The seating was so arranged to immerse our guest of honor and her flock in a truly captivating experience. I sat side by side with her, while Uncle Zale and Sister Zizi sat side by side, facing us. The ten gladiators found comfort along a long table, out of earshot of where we were seated. This unusual seating arrangement was to obviate eavesdropping on our chat with the mystery girl.

And the time came for the introduction. And as soon as I began presenting my sister and the husband to her, the mystery girl hastily took over, giving a detailed account of Sister Zizi and Uncle Zale. She mentioned the schools and colleges they attended and their places of work, as well as the names of their parents. She went on, even, to tell them about the recent trip they made to the countryside. Then and there, she began introducing herself.

"Well, as you have christened me, I am the mystery girl; but you will very soon, find out that there is nothing mystery about me. I am just a tenant of the blue planet like any one of you here," she explained in a euphonious voice that appeared to have enhanced the credibleness of what she was saying.

"Accompanying me to this important summit—or is it lovefest?—are eternal friends of mine, who get on swimmingly and famously with me. I move in the same circles with them, through thick and thin. They are ten in number, and I already know that you've nicknamed them *The Ten Gladiators*. Yes, as the name rightly suggests, they are only supporting characters of the unfolding storyline of which I am the empress, and your darling boy, Zaza, is the emperor."

As she mentioned my name, she paused for a while, gazed at me, and released a contagious smile that infected me with heavenly bliss.

"I am very delighted to be here to learn and unlearn," she continued. "Unlearning is the surest way to purge our civilization of the preconceptions undermining the creation of an Eldorado in every hamlet of our universe," she explained.

"Our people are living in abject poverty in the midst of abundant wealth. We have mortgaged our wealth for want, devotedly worshipping scarcity in almost every province of human subsistence: in our homes, in our workplaces, in our schools, in our health facilities, and even in our places of worship," she bewailed, looking utterly disillusioned.

"We have poisoned our politics and reduced it to hate, blackmailing, vote-buying, and money-making, turning it into a communion table for family and friends to celebrate their ill-gotten wealth," she lamented.

"But it should not be so," she countered, pointing at the region's copious human and natural resources.

"Every state in our region has abundant human and natural resources. Every state in our region also has abundant poverty and miseries to nurse," she noted in wonderment and abruptly ended her speech.

As she sat down, Uncle Zale took over from where she left, assertively unveiling the economic jewels of the region and lamentably cataloging the woes and tribulations of its inhabitants.

"I entirely agree with you, my dear," Uncle Zale began, as he took a roll-call of the seven states that conspire and contradict, to sum up the amazing Sunrise Hemisphere: Indomitable Kingdom of Zoland, Venomous Empire of Voberia, Cooperative Republic of Yonta, Commonwealth of Tozan, Homeland of Wongo, Communality of Pogan, and Union of Motolands. He painstakingly audited the economic potential of each of them.

"We have almost every precious stone and vast deposits of hydrocarbons in this region, making us present a geological paradox, hard to unlock," he noted with pride, "yet we cannot generate the needed power to light our homes and drive our industries to bring comfort to our people," he grieved in disappointment. He laid the blame squarely at the doorstep of political managers of the region and called for a total overhaul of the political architecture of the region.

However, the distressed and disappointed mood in which he was speaking suddenly transmuted into a cheerful spirit as he began beaming in broad smiles. Perhaps, this was occasioned by the rapt attention with which the mystery girl was receiving his political sermon. Unexpectedly, Uncle Zale changed the point of discussion and formally welcomed the guest of honor and her associates to his abode with the popping of champagne. This transformed the setting from a seeming political rally ground to a social gathering. And all the courses in meals, and tots of drinks associated with partying, began to flow.

All were dining and wining, while a repertoire of soul-searching delicious music was dutifully at work. The mystery girl had no excuse but to join in the merrymaking. So did her ten gladiators. They ate, drank, and danced. Uncle Zale and Sister Zizi also participated effectively, just as I did. And as the jollification got to a crescendo with intensified babbling, the mystery girl dropped another bombshell.

"And where is beautiful Zifi?" she politely inquired. "I will like to see her and have a word with her," she pleaded. As soon as she mentioned Zifi's name, Zifi suddenly appeared. And right away, she beckoned Zifi to her side. And the two got engaged in the exchange of confidences. They spent a long time, heartily enjoying the talkfest as if they knew each other for years.

While this was happening, I became nervous and worried. And I could also notice worry boldly registered on the faces of Sister Zizi and Uncle Zale. Possibly, we might be sharing a common worry; a worry over the subject matter of the mystery girl's heart-to-heart with Zifi. "Is Zifi divulging any information that could subvert the mystery girl's burning desire to tie the knot with me?" That was one of my two fears. The other was the possibility of the mystery girl disclosing a scrap of information that could ruin the cordial relationship between Zifi and me and, indeed, the entire Zale family.

However, the pillow-talk ended with the two heartily laughing and hugging. Surprisingly, the mystery girl got out of her seat and escorted smiling Zifi to sit among the ten gladiators. There, too, Zifi got companions, enthusiastically talking and sharing jokes with the Amazonian beauty queens.

The jamboree continued and the small talks, crisscrossing uncommon but uncontroversial matters, continued until we all became dog-tired. The time had now come for the mystery girl and her following to begin a homebound journey. And she announced it, expressing a profound appreciation for the wonderful reception accorded to them. Then, she began spraying gifts on us all. I had mine; Zifi had hers; Sister Zizi and Uncle Zale had theirs; even young Zito had his.

After the tsunami of gifts that swallowed our expectations, the mystery girl went to Sister Zizi and Uncle Zale, whispered something in their ears, and they all advertised winsome smiles. She shook their hands and bade them goodbye. Then, came the turn of Zifi; she embraced her, whispered something in her ear, and released an 'au-revoir' in an emotional tone. Next was young Zito; she held his hand, asked him to be a good boy, and promised him more toys. And finally, my turn. She came to me eyeball-to-eyeball, hugged me, and gave me an emotion-arousing sweet, erotic French kiss while all were watching.

After successfully performing the leave-taking rite, she instantly left with her contingent of stoutly built nice-looking ladies. All was over now, and we also left the party ground, extremely exhausted but exceedingly contemplative.

The next day, we gathered for a debriefing session. And the foremost item on the agenda was the undreamed-of gifts. Uncle Zale led the way and we all followed, carefully itemizing the gifts the mystery girl had poured on us. They were beyond-belief and indescribable, running from pricey, classy ego goods, spruced up with unbelievable amounts of cash to commonplace items like a tube of toothpaste and children's toys. Everyone had a cash gift, even Uncle Zale; and unsurprisingly, I had the lion's share, followed by Zifi.

The other issue that took much of our time was the feverish talkfest Zifi celebrated with the mystery girl. We wanted to know the subject matter of their one-on-one but Zifi turned down our request, utterly refusing to disclose the centerpiece of their conversation. She only laughed and apologized for gate-crashing the party. She, however, expressed great delight for meeting the mystery girl, describing her as a new-found soulmate.

In spite of this, Zifi continued her visitations to our house, with even heightened intensity, assisting in the household tasks, and trading her usual gorgeous and mischievous jokes with me. However, she had refrained from positioning herself as the mother of my future child as she used to do. Instead, she began addressing me as brother and relaying to me messages from the mystery girl, with whom she had been in constant communication.

Uncle Zale and Sister Zizi had noticed that our lovebirds' project had developed irreparable cracks and was a candidate for imminent liquidation. And they seemed not to bother. Instead, they focused their attention on unlocking the identity of the mystery girl.

As the search for the nationality of the mystery girl continued, Uncle Zale decided to give me a brief classroom lesson on the uniqueness of the Sunrise Hemisphere. This was to help me carefully navigate the seeming meandering lanes of the marriage proposal the mystery girl had floated.

"The Sunrise Hemisphere is an exceptional landmass that is highly homogenous culturally. All the seven states in the region speak the same language, with no variations. Citizens of the states look alike in appearance, and their nationalities can only be known by their names. The names of citizens of each state begin with the first letter of the name of their state. This explains why the name of every Zolandese starts with the letter Z, and all Voberians have their names beginning with the letter V.

"Interstate marriage is a taboo in the region. The punishment for breaking this cultural legislation is banishment. As a result, this cultural taboo is devoutly observed and has never been broken. This explains why there are no half-blooded citizens in any state in the region; we are all pure-blooded. And this is one of the unique selling points of our branded pride, which we arrogantly auction at international gatherings.

"The capital cities of the states also have unique names. They take the first two letters of the name of the state and box it up with the word "city". As a result, the capital of Zoland, as you are aware, is called Zo City; that of Voberia, Vo City; Yonta, Yo City; Tozan, To City; Wongo, Wo City; Pogan, Po City; and Motolands, Mo City.

"Interestingly, the frontiers of the states are distinctively delineated by geographical features such as rivers, seas, lakes, lagoons, mountains, and valleys. Regrettably, claims to these transboundary geographical features, which are very rich in mineral resources, have always been the source of interstate rivalries, tensions, and wars in the region."

Uncle Zale concluded his tutorial, drawing my attention to the beauty of the linguistic homogeneity of the Sunrise Hemisphere but lamented that this enthralling beauty had been desecrated by a cultural decree, outlawing interstate marriage.

"A cultural decree? And will it be, from here, my problems begin?" I thought long and hard as I pondered over the mystery girl and her reluctance to disclose her identity.

"I know next to nothing about her to conjecture her nationality; not even her name or her phone number," I kept grumbling. "Being a native of Sunrise Hemisphere, and a true devotee of cultural values, her name will surely give away her nationality," I reasoned out, wondering how I could stumble upon the elusive name.

Meanwhile, the mystery girl had stopped visiting me; and also ceased calling me on the phone. However, she regularly sent me gifts and love-laden messages through Zifi. It appeared Zifi had elected herself to be my official envoy to the mystery girl, faithfully negotiating love contracts and signing love treaties on my behalf.

Chapter Seven
The Invitation of the Zale Family to the King's Palace

As the confusion engulfing the nationality and realness of the mystery girl continued, Uncle Zale had a strange and surprising invitation to attend a special ceremony at His Majesty King Zozozo Palace. Also, included in the invitation were Sister Zizi, Zifi, Zito, and me. Uncle Zale became dumbfounded because he did not know the nature of the ceremony. Moreover, he was not a politician and could not fathom why he and his family should be invited to the political powerhouse of the kingdom.

So, he began looking out for an answer, consulting people in corridors of power. And at last, the answer came. The occasion-in-wait was the official opening of the Voberian Embassy in Zo City. Responding to the peace overtures, His Highness King Zozozo of the Indomitable Kingdom of Zoland made to the Venomous Empire of Voberia during the last Zado Festival, Vo City agreed to renew ties with Zo City at the ambassadorial level. And His Imperial Highness, Emperor Vovovo had decided to visit

Zo City to hold bilateral talks with his Zolandese counterpart before officially opening the embassy himself.

Uncle Zale summoned us to a meeting and broke the news to us. While I was so excited by the lifetime opportunity to visit His Majesty's imposing palace, I could notice worry, boldly inscribed in uppercase, on the face of Uncle Zale. Sister Zizi too did not get carried away by the news. She received it with cautious optimism. As for Zifi, she was in seventh heaven, extremely happy.

"But who knows me and my family in Zolandese politics to extend such an important invitation to us?" Uncle Zale began questioning, as he critically scrutinized the invitation card, examining the spellings of the names on it.

"What connection do I have with Voberia to be invited to attend the opening of its embassy in Zo City?" he repeatedly asked, with the invitation card, still seeking asylum in his hand.

"And my three-year-old Zito, what role is he going to play in the opening of an embassy?" he touchingly questioned without venturing to guess a response.

Sister Zizi quickly countered her husband, saying, "It will be a history-making moment for Zito, a unique opportunity for him to tour His Majesty's huge palace."

"Oh, how can a three-year-old boy tour a heavily guarded palace?" Uncle Zale chimed in with a smile and sarcastically added, "Surely, Zito will be His Majesty's guest of honor, and His Majesty himself will take him around the palace."

We all burst into irresistible spontaneous laughter and immediately turned our attention to drawing up a rock-hard line-up for the seven-days-away ceremony. The outfit to wear on this auspicious occasion was our main concern. We wanted to appear charmingly sleek and cute. The wardrobes of Uncle Zale and Sister Zizi as well as that of Zifi met the high bar dressing code we had set for ourselves. Zito and I became the odd ones out. It meant His Majesty's magnificent palace would be out of our reach. However, Uncle Zale instantly went to town and procured the looked-for trendy dresses for us.

"All is set for the rare opportunity to set eyes on the two most popular political heavyweights in the Sunrise Hemisphere," I said to myself as I journeyed on the tracks of contemporary history into the past and discovered that the two political titans were not compatible and never seeing eye to eye. I also found out that in every encounter between the two, the Voberian kaiser always held sway over the Zolandese khan. I, therefore, had very high expectations of the approaching summit of the two rulers, who shared nothing in common than enmity.

Finally, the day for the ceremony arrived, and we promptly found ourselves in the splendid conference room of the magnificent King Zozozo Palace. From little Zito to Uncle Zale and Sister Zizi, through Zifi to me, we were all glowingly decked out, looking extremely impeccable and exceedingly immaculate. And as soon as we arrived, we were escorted to seats in the front row, bearing our names. As we later discovered, we were seated among VIPs: ministers of state, members of parliament, and members of the diplomatic corps.

As I got seated and surveyed the entire perimeter of the conference room and its state-of-the-art accessories, I could imagine the unnumbered meetings it had hosted. I could also imagine the myriad of secrets it had kept within its four walls. I dug into the past and stumbled upon the popular saying, "Conference rooms are secret keepers," and wondered if any high-profile secret would find a storage space on the walls of the conference room after the soon-to-be-held meeting between the two heads of state.

And while the mind's eye was on duty, feverishly striving to conquer its own curiosity, out of the public-address system boomed the announcement, "Ladies and Gentlemen, His Majesty King Zozozo of the Indomitable Kingdom of Zoland, and His Highness Emperor Vovovo of the Venomous Empire of Voberia." Suddenly, a tidal wave of pin-drop silence consumed us, and we were all up on our feet, even three-year-old Zito. And there emerged His Majesty King Zozozo and His Highness Emperor Vovovo on the podium. They were accompanied by their aides-de-camp.

Surprisingly, standing beside the Voberian Emperor was the mystery girl. We could not believe our eyes. We stole a panicking look at one another and recoiled into stunned silence. The two tsars were now ready to speak on the outcome of the closed-door meeting they had just held. And we were all ears. First to speak was the host, His Majesty King Zozozo.

He began in a free-flowing, glowing language, welcoming Emperor Vovovo and his entourage to the Indomitable Kingdom of Zoland, describing the visit as historic.

"This is a history-making visit, which has already found a conspicuous place in the Guinness Book of Records," he asserted, noting that this was the first time in two hundred years that a Voberian Emperor had visited Zoland.

"And on my behalf, and on behalf of all Zolandese, I warmly welcome you, Your Highness, and your entourage to Zoland. As I stated at the recent Zado Festival, the frontiers of human progress are fast changing, and if we continue doing things the same old way, we shall be drowned by the rainstorms of change. We have to learn new things to bring on-board the refinement needed for progress and development to thrive in our countries. Equally, we have to unlearn old things to clear the barriers to the change, we inevitably need to chart the path to peace and development.

"I am happy to announce that at the just-ended meeting with His Highness Emperor Vovovo, Zoland and Voberia have taken sweeping measures to begin the unlearning process to bring peace and advancement to our people," he declared with delight and began enumerating the measures.

"As a first step, Zoland and Voberia have restored full diplomatic relations after two hundred years. And Emperor Vovovo is here today to officially open the Voberian embassy in Zo City. We have also opened transportation links between our two states. Additionally, we have agreed to normalize trade and cultural relations," he revealed, as he rained praises on Emperor Vovovo for doing what his predecessors could not do in two centuries.

"Your Highness, permit me to say this. You are a trailblazer, a trendsetter in transnational politics. You have a deep ocean of love for humanity. And today, you have demonstrated this through the forward-looking decisions you have taken to bring the daylight of hope to the homes and hearts of millions in our region. Surely, there is a special place in history for you. History will honor you. The present and future generations of our two countries owe you a deep and lasting debt of gratitude."

The Zolandese monarch concluded his speech, urging political and business managers in the two countries to take advantage of the wide range of opportunities presented by the new wind of change blowing across Zoland and Voberia to improve the living conditions of their people.

Now came the turn of His Highness Emperor Vovovo of Voberia to speak. Flanked by the mystery girl and a military officer, and in a delicious vocal sound, he began his speech.

"Many thanks to you, Your Majesty, and indeed, to the wonderful people of Zoland for the rousing welcome you have given me and my delegation to your beautiful country. We were so moved by the incredible warmth of your reception. Your deep and friendly welcome touched our souls without words. Indeed, we are very grateful for gifting us an occasion filled with moments of joy, pride, color, laughter, and good company.

"For two hundred years, no Voberian emperor had set foot on Zoland. It was sacrilegious to do so, and the punishment was more than a death sentence. But here I am today, breaking that deep-seated cultural taboo and heartily enjoying the hospitality of the Zolandese king and his people. Everything has its time. It is true; and now is the time for this too.

"Yes, I have offered myself to be the sacrificial lamb to be slaughtered on the altar of archaic traditions to bring the fundamental change needed to propel the peace and development of our region. It is no secret that our people are living in chronic and endemic poverty, ignorance, and disease. It is also no secret that unless we embrace change as our new vehicle for conducting our affairs, we cannot reach the destination of peace and development we direly need to bring comfort to our people.

"However, it takes a certain amount of madness and courage to turn back on old ways of doing things to create a new future. And as we begin this journey here today, to create a fulfilling future for our region, many of us, especially Your Majesty and I, will be portrayed as madmen on a mission to divert the course of tradition and history.

"Why should Zoland dine with Voberia, its public enemy number one? This is the question they will be asking. However, beneath this, seeming, simple question is the more complex question, 'What dividends has the 200-year diplomatic boycott brought to the people of Zoland and Voberia?' Is it not poverty and want, hungrily packaged in retrogression and beautifully wrapped in hate?

"Your Majesty, the new wind of change blowing over our two countries is an infectious wind that will infect all states in our Sunrise Hemisphere and pull down all cultural taboos and beliefs undercutting development. The idea is to unite all our seven nations and integrate our economies to effectively compete with other regions of the world. Will it not be a nice idea for us to have a United States of Sunrise Hemisphere?

"Today, I will be opening our embassy here in your beautiful capital city. And this will mark the beginning of the lively socio-economic interaction between the citizens of our two countries. There will be free movement of people and goods across our borders, making it possible for our people to enjoy the luxury of variety and choice. Your Majesty, I am using your country, the Indomitable Kingdom of Zoland as the launching pad for the unity we so desired in this region. From here, I will be transmitting peace signals to other states in the region, and, hopefully, they will soon be on the same bandwagon with us.

"Thank you, and God bless us all."

A perfect speech for a perfect occasion. And, undoubtedly, it was His Majesty King Zozozo himself who led the audience to give the Voberian emperor an electrifying standing ovation. I enjoyed every bit of the speech. It was colorful and moving, stirring the urge for peace, unity, and development.

From here, we all moved in a convoy to an imposing structure, not far-off from His Majesty's palace, for a brief ceremony to formally open the Voberian Embassy and immediately returned to the palace for a luncheon in honor of the visiting Voberian sovereign. While responding to the toast proposed by King Zozozo at the luncheon, the Voberian emperor introduced our perceived mystery girl as Crown Princess Vovona, the only child of his and the heiress-apparent to the imperial throne. The emperor credited the daughter for being the brain behind the normalization of relations between Zoland and Voberia.

Our supposed mystery girl, whose true identity had now been revealed as Voberian Crown Princess Vovona, defied protocol and took the lunch together with us, heartily chatting with us, to the amazement of all, even her father and King Zozozo. In a unique photo op at the end of the lunch, we took pictures with Crown Princess Vovona together with her father and King Zozozo. During the photo session, Princess Vovona was, at a point, seen carrying little Zito. When all was over, Princess Vovona, exhibiting her usual self, splashed divine and priceless gifts on us, bade us cheerful and lingering goodbye, and left with her father and his entourage. Surprisingly, the ten gladiators were not with her, instead, she was accompanied by uniformed men and women.

The following day, we became the talking point in the country, as our pictures with the visiting Voberian emperor and his princess, together with the Zolandese king, dominated the front pages of major newspapers with screaming headlines. "Five Unknown Zolandese Steal the Show," thundered the *Zo City Herald*, while the *Zoland Times* trumpeted the presence of Zito in the picture with the headline, "Three-Year-Old Zolandese Wins the Heart of Voberian Emperor and His Princess." As for the ubiquitous *Zo City Post*, it roared with the headline, "The Zale Family Sends Peace Message to Voberia."

We were inundated with calls from relatives, friends, and loved ones. They wanted to know how we made it, attending that big event and crowning it, taking pictures with political colossuses like His Majesty King Zozozo, His Imperial Highness Emperor Vovovo, and Princess Vovona. We could not offer any palpable answer except saying, we were invited. The electronic media, too, did not spare us. Radio and television stations called on us for interviews, but we declined.

Even, His Majesty King Zozozo invited us for an audience at his palace. He found it hard to understand how ordinary Zolandese citizens like us could dribble our way through the barriers of deep distrust and strict protocol to become trusted allies of the top leadership of mighty Voberia. Uncle Zale only told the king that Princess Vovona was a family friend. However, His Majesty did not go further to probe how the friendship was developed.

Apparently, it was Princess Vovona who made the arrangement for our invitation to the ceremony as special dignitaries. She arranged for the photo op too. Her father, Emperor Vovovo was aware of this as she had been mentioning us to him. The Zolandese authorities were duly informed of our coming as VVIPs and had, accordingly, extended the necessary courtesies to us, seating us in the front row among dignitaries.

Three days later, Princess Vovona called Uncle Zale on the phone and arranged to visit us over the weekend. How she inexplicably got Uncle Zale's phone number was not unusual to us, as we were already aware of her exploits in fathomless, thrilling mysteries. However, Uncle Zale was very excited to hear about her proposed visit and instantly broke the news to us.

Straightaway, Sister Zizi called me and addressed me as 'Emperor-in-Waiting.'

"Sister, 'Emperor-in-Waiting' for which empire?" I objected unwaveringly and added, "You know our Zoland is a kingdom and cannot have an emperor. Moreover, you are aware that we are not from the royal family and cannot inherit the throne," I warm-heartedly lectured my sister.

"Though you are not an emperor-in-waiting, you should consider yourself a candidate for emperor-in-waiting," Uncle Zale explained, as he joined the conversation. "The venerable heiress apparent to the powerful Voberian imperial throne has proposed to marry you," he reminded me, and said, "If the proposal finally eventuates into marriage, then you surely become an emperor-in-waiting."

"That is the new label you are going to wear now, heavy as it is, you have to live up to its responsibilities," Sister Zizi advised, and we all dissolved into enduring laughter.

"Oh no, 'Emperor in-Waiting' will not be the right label for you, Zaza," Uncle Zale tactfully chimed in. "It will rather be 'Emperor Consort in-Waiting," he pointed out, citing established traditional royal practices across the globe.

After haggling and squabbling over the yet-to-be-confirmed designation to be embossed on me, we shifted our attention to Crown Princess Vovona and her impending visit. Having been overwhelmed by how her sponsored invitation to His Majesty's palace had lifted us from oblivion to the glare of publicity, we agreed to give her an imperishable treat.

Uncle Zale had an elaborate program for the visit. He invited our parents from the countryside, as well as a few close friends. He procured the services of the best caterer in town to provide relishing, heavenly cuisine. He also engaged the celebrated National Symphony Orchestra to provide lush, uplifting classical music befitting a monarch.

At the agreed time, we were securely seated with the invitees, and suddenly Princess Vovona arrived, all dolled up for the occasion, and, as usual, in the company of her ten gladiators. Surprisingly, after exchanging greetings, she went straight to my mother, had a brief chat with her, and retired to her seat. How she managed to identify my mother among the pack could only be one of the marvels in her always-on-duty baggage of mysteries.

It was an interactive gathering. Protocol was thrown into the dustbin of social intercourse. We mingled and commingled, chatting, eating, drinking, and joyously enjoying soul-searching renditions from the orchestra. Soon, all was over, and the princess had to leave. She guardedly performed her customary goodbye ritual, smiling, hugging, and shaking hands.

Predictably, presentation of gifts took place. However, on this occasion, the river of benevolence flowed in a reversed direction to the path of the princess, crowning her a beneficiary instead of a benefactor, as had always been the case. For the first time, she received gifts from us. Uncle Zale presented her with a precious Zolandese gold artifact. Nevertheless, before her departure, she told Uncle Zale to expect gifts from the Voberian Embassy in Zo City from her father to our parents.

When all had left, my astonished mom called me and asked me, how I managed to win the heart of that divine jewel, glittering with untouchable inner beauty, strikingly spelt out in charm, compassion, and graciousness. "And will she be willing to visit us at our humble abode in the village?" my mother prayed, looking up to the heavens for an answer.

Then, she fixed her motherly eyes firmly on me and continued her interrogation. "Will her father, the very powerful emperor of Voberia, allow her only daughter to marry someone from Zoland?" Mom wondered as she began a history session with me, highlighting the interstate wars, acrimonies, and rivalries that had, for years, been the pastime of the region. Her questions flowed and flowed until I convinced her to expect the unexpected, and that politics is the shrewdest game of unpredictability man had ever invented.

Chapter Eight
Voberian Emperor in Search of Regional Peace

As part of his desire to clothe the entire region in peace, the Voberian emperor methodically tied together a blueprint, he christened the "Comprehensive Plan for Peace and Development of the Sunrise Hemisphere." The document, which detailed a roadmap to ending all interstate conflicts in the region, was intended to usher in a new era of peace, unity, and development in the hemisphere. The ultimate goal of the plan was to integrate all economies in the region into an economic union, and eventually progress to a political union.

Emperor Vovovo therefore, embarked on a regional tour, painstakingly selling the idea to his fellow heads of state. However, the plan was flatly rejected, as it was interpreted as a ploy by Voberia to revive and entrench its centuries-old hegemony over the rest of the states in the region. Even, its new-found ally, Zoland, rejected the plan.

Voberia is the largest state in the hemisphere, covering more than fifty percent of the landmass. It has the biggest economy, accounting for nearly sixty percent of the region's

Gross Domestic Product. Four out of every ten people found in the region are Voberians. In addition, the country has a large number of first-class universities, churning out highly qualified professionals in medicine, science, law, finance, business, engineering, education, and other disciplines. Voberians enjoy free education from kindergarten to university. Undoubtedly, the country has an unbelievable literacy rate of nearly 90%, the second highest in the region.

Furthermore, Voberia has a sophisticated military-industrial complex with a standing force of nearly one million soldiers, made up of the army, navy, air force, space force, and cyber force as well as a powerful defense industry, supplying an array of the latest deadly weapons. As a result, Voberian soldiers are extremely fearsome on land, in the air, in water, in space, and in cyber. Voberia has for centuries colonized and recolonized states in the region. For this reason, political and diplomatic overtures of Voberia are always seen with a jaundiced eye and taken with a pinch of salt.

Having had his plan rejected, Emperor Vovovo went back to the drawing board to re-strategize. And this time, he found solace in soft power diplomacy, deploying sports as a unique selling proposition for re-branding his peace project and carefully marketing it to his peers. Consequently, he organized a Sports Festival in Vo City, attended by all the states in the region. As would be expected, Princess Vovona used her influence to ensure that I attended the tournament as an official of Team Zoland.

The two-week games, assembled more than five thousand sportsmen and women, competing in various sporting disciplines—athletics, boxing, basketball, volleyball, hockey, wrestling, cricket, football, weightlifting, tennis, and rugby. The whole-hearted reception accorded the athletes and their officials was beyond compare. They were housed in posh hotels and were given celebratory meals throughout the tournament. The athletes had at their disposal, hi-tech facilities for training. In attendance at each of the events, were cheering crowds who sold out indiscriminate support to the athletes.

Though the sporting events were fiercely contested, bringing to the fore national pride and prejudice, they were so arranged that the athletes from different states had the opportunity to regularly interact and develop friendships. There were a variety of entertainment programs from which the athletes could choose to recreate themselves. It was a combination of a sportsfest and a lovefest, and we enjoyed every bit of it.

His Imperial Highness was always around, throughout the tournament, to personally present medals to the winners. All the heads of state in the region attended the impressive closing session, which featured an assortment of cultural displays from each of the seven states in the region, beautifully spelling out unity in diversity. And the glowing expression on the faces of the political overlords, glaringly summed up the breadth and depth of their joy.

The over-thrilled heads of state consulted among themselves and agreed to make the sports festival an annual event to rotate between the states in the region. For the spectacular performance, it put up at the tournament, the heads of state unanimously selected the Union of Motolands, the tiniest nation in the region, to host the next games.

At the end of it all, it was all smiles for the athletes as they were presented with gifts of expensive Voberian souvenirs. For the medal winners, they did not only carry home medals and souvenirs but also took home cash prizes. And a scoop of journalists from all seven nations were around to give the festival the deserved coverage, showcasing Emperor Vovovo's Voberia as a pacesetter in efforts to bring peace, unity, and development to the region.

The successful holding of the games raised the diplomatic profile of the Voberian emperor and recast the country as the center of gravity of affairs in the region. Armed with this red-hot opportunity, Emperor Vovovo began another round of diplomatic maneuvers, shuttling between national capitals, to sell his peace and development plan to his peers.

His first port of call was the tiny nation of the Union of Motolands, the host for the next regional sports festival. Motolands is the most highly educated nation in the region, with a literacy rate of nearly 100%. It practices a mixture of democracy and technocracy. Though it operates democracy, with a ritual of periodic elections, higher qualifications are set for the eligibility to contest elections in the country. While Ph.D. is the minimum educational qualification for contesting presidential and vice-presidential elections, that of parliamentary elections is a master's degree. In addition to the educational qualifications, another important requirement for presidential and parliamentary candidacy is a proof of distinguished career in business, public service, military, police, academia, agriculture, religion, and other callings in society.

To concretize competency in every province of governance, elected officials in Motolands are made to painstakingly recruit experts and professionals to perform key government functions. Motolands, thus, operates a hybrid of democracy and technocracy with the vision of reaching the destination of a pure meritocracy, where the ablest are in charge without the influence of political mafias or special interest groups.

With the celebration of the honor of being selected to host the next regional games still at fever-pitch in the country, Emperor Vovovo did not find it difficult to convince President Mototo of Motolands to whole-heartedly embrace his peace plan. In a communique announcing the endorsement of the plan, President Mototo hailed the peace plan as a catalyst to drive the development aspirations of the region and improve the living conditions of the people. The endorsement was extensively carried by the media throughout the region.

From Motolands, the emperor went to the Cooperative Republic of Yonta, the only parliamentary democracy in the region with full-fledged democratic institutions. Here, Emperor Vovovo, in the presence of his host, Prime Minister Yonyon, had the rare opportunity to address the Yontanian parliament to explain his peace plan. The speech touched the hearts of the Yontanian lawmakers, who overwhelmingly voted to endorse the peace plan.

At the same time, two other states, the Indomitable Kingdom of Zoland, and the Homeland of Wongo, without much persuasion, announced their endorsement of the plan. The Homeland of Wongo is a presidential democracy, famously known for its strict adherence to the principles and practice of the rule of law, while Zoland is a monarchy with an elected parliament. With these two countries endorsing the peace plan, Emperor Vovovo was now left with only the Commonwealth of Tozan, and the Communality of Pogan, the two hardline states in the region, to sway.

Tozan is a pure theocratic state beautifully packaged in autocracy. It has only one religion known as Tozanla, and all Tozanians practice this faith. The constitution of the country is derived from the holy scripture of the Tozanla religion.

Tozan operates a one-man government. The president is the head of state, head of government, head of the legislature, head of the judiciary, as well as the spiritual head of the Tozanla religion. His speeches and sermons are laws, strictly enforced. It is believed that God communicates directly with the spiritual leader. As a result, insulting the spiritual leader is interpreted as insulting God. This is a grievous offense that carries a death sentence.

After God, there is no one more powerful in the world than the spiritual leader. His birthday is the biggest national commemoration in the country. It is a public holiday, observed with elaborate cultural displays, sporting activities, fireworks, and other forms of entertainment. On that day, women are not allowed to go to the kitchen. It is the men who prepare the 'holy meal' for the sacred occasion. It is a criminal offense to travel outside the country without an exeat, duly signed by the spiritual leader, himself. No doubt, Tozan is a police state.

The Communality of Pogan, on the other hand, is an unholy trinity of kakistocracy, kleptocracy, and khakistocracy. And in the name of kakistocracy which breeds incompetency, and of kleptocracy which mass-produces thieves, and of khakistocracy, which swears in military dictatorships, Pogan has been raided of all its financial resources, leaving the entire population wretchedly poor and mournfully unhappy.

The country's leaders are extremely corrupt, using political power to profusely siphon the country's wealth. They misappropriate state funds, indulge in large-scale kickbacks, and other forms of inducement, exporting the bulk of their ill-gotten money to banks abroad. Poganian heads of state are always the richest people in the country, and, in fact, richer than the country they rule. Their obsession for amassing wealth is so acute that they are often referred to as 'walking vaults.' At any time anywhere and everywhere, a Poganian senior government official has a large sum of cash on hand. A Poganian president could take the phone and order the Central Bank to bring as much as half-a-million US dollars in cash, and the order would be carried out within minutes.

The national economy is under the beck and call of the president. He determines the supply and disbursement of all financial resources. He controls every industry in the country. Poganian leaders are notorious for making prodigal expenses, embarking on ostentatious projects, and leading flamboyant lifestyles. General Popog once spent an eye-watering US $38,000 on a meal with his family in a restaurant. He, as well, spent a whopping US $3million on his daughter's wedding, attended by 2,500 guests, serving hand-picked champagnes costing between $150 and $750 per bottle.

On the contrary, Pogan is the least developed nation in the region. In fact, it is one of the worst places in the universe to raise a child. There is widespread poverty and severe starvation. Children eat hungry food and are severely malnourished. Immorality has contaminated every dominion of national life. Prostitution is a lucrative industry and, in fact, the only option for the survival of young women and girls. For the young men and boys, they stake their survival on robbery and the sale of drugs and other contraband goods.

The socio-economic environment in the country is morally rotten to the extent that stealing is no longer seen as a crime but a legal business with recruitment agencies, while bribery is considered an accepted norm in business management. The cost of living is so high that people deliberately commit crimes to go to prison in order to survive, since within the prison walls, they are assured of free meals provided by the state.

Nothing appears to hold together in the country as anarchy reigns everywhere. The teaching and learning environment cannot hold together. The salary-denied, de-motivated teachers and the drug-addicted, rowdy students always clash, resulting in rampant strikes and demonstrations. Press freedom is off-limits here, and citizens only subsist on information hand-outs from the strictly controlled state media. Ironically, Pogan is potentially one of the wealthiest countries in the region. It has abundant mineral and hydrocarbon deposits, a variety of food and cash crops, and a web of freshwater bodies crisscrossing the length and breadth of the country.

Pogan and Tozan were now the inaccessible and unnavigable rivers left to cross. The task ahead appeared exceedingly hazardous and seemingly impossible. Nonetheless, Emperor Vovovo marshaled his accouterment of diplomatic ritual and headed to the two countries, arriving first in Tozan. He was given a rousing welcome in To City, Tozan's dizzying chief city, set ablaze with overflowing human numbers and foothills of retired industrial machinery, and immediately went into talks with the Tozanian Supreme Spiritual Leader, Tozaza. After more than four hours, the two heads of state emerged, completely deflated of the oxygen of the shine and vigor that ushered them into the talks. No communique was issued, and neither of the leaders spoke to the media. Wearing an expression of disappointment, the visiting Voberian emperor instantly flew out.

From To City, Emperor Vovovo went straight to Po City, the Poganian capital, where he was received by the Poganian military leader, General Popog. The two engaged in talks for less than two hours, after which a communique was issued announcing the endorsement of the peace plan by the Communality of Pogan. An unexpected diplomatic victory, it was, and the Voberian monarch celebrated it granting extensive interviews to the media across the region. Surprisingly, as he was celebrating the victory, Tozanian Supreme Spiritual Leader Tozaza announced his acceptance of the peace plan. Emperor Vovovo was very excited about the dramatic turn of events. Though all the seven states in the region had now jumped on his peace bandwagon, he would not declare it a mission accomplished, until the peace initiative was translated into

a working document, formally signed and showily launched
by the regional heads of state.

Chapter Nine
The Ground-Breaking Summit
of Heads of State

In consultation with his Zolandese counterpart, Emperor Vovovo called for the holding of a summit of heads of state of the region in Zo City to officially inaugurate the peace project. The magnificent King Zozozo Palace was chosen as the venue for this all-important meeting of the political heavyweights. Elaborate preparations were made to dress up the occasion in an enduring pageantry. A few days before the summit, the Zolandese capital was lit up with flags of the seven nations and portraits of their heads of state. Leading cultural troupes drawn from the seven states converged on the Zolandese capital to rehearse, and jointly put on performances to depict the rich cultural heritage of the region.

I had the singular honor to witness the opening ceremony of the two-day summit, and it was a once-in-a-life-time event to celebrate. The color, pomp, and excitement that punctuated the confluence of the various presentations that pulled together to form the ceremony, warmed the heart, lifted the spirit, and stirred the soul. The well-choreographed cultural performances on display, beautifully conspired with the inspiring speeches churned out by the political managers to stamp a lingering memory on the event. One by one, the seven heads of state expressed their candid opinion on the soon-to-come moment of truth for the region. However, it was the host, His Majesty King Zozozo, who began it all, with a soul-stirring welcome address.

"Your Excellencies, Ladies, and Gentlemen, I am highly delighted to welcome you all to our humble abode. Here, we do not have the sprawling, towering buildings that are the icons of national capitals. We do not have the flashy cars that draw the dividing line between the poor and the rich. We do not have the mega shops, the supermarkets, and the giant shopping malls that determine the fanatic consuming patterns of capitalism. No. Ours is a simple world of bicycles, a simple world of creating something out of nothing, a simple world of brotherliness, submerged in humility, tolerance, and patience. Ours is a pure Zolandese world of sowing love together and harvesting hope and joy together. At the end of your stay here, your attitude toward the environment will not be the same; your perception of poverty will not be the same; your understanding of human values will not be the same.

"You have come to a world where people are creating green vegetation out of gray deserts. You are in a world where people are turning naked poverty into stinking riches. You are in a world where people consider everything as a resource, even misfortune, and use it to propel themselves to greater heights. Our official currency, here, is patience, and our official language is love. So, speak love and transact all your businesses in patience.

"As we gather here as managers of our people's destinies, we are haunted by the mistakes of the known past, and motivated by the fears of the unknown future to invent a working formula to change the destiny of our region. History has already pronounced a verdict on us. We have failed our people. But it is from the ruins of the failure that we shall erect the mighty edifice of hope for our hemisphere. I am galvanized by the self-assured looks on your faces and propelled by the meandering course of history that our region's hour of refinement has, at last, dawned.

"We are going to pool our resources together and enjoy the synergy of numbers. We are going to make available our different cultures and enjoy the beauty of diversity. We are going to unite our economies and enjoy the fellowship of unity. However, the calculable numbers, the manifold diversity, and the blessed fellowship will come to naught, if we do not surrender part of our sovereignty. In a comity of nations, the propelling principle is 'give and take.' We have to give out part of our national pride and our national identity to take away the beauty and abundance that unity brings."

After abundantly extolling the sterling virtues of unity, His Majesty King Zozozo declared the summit of heads of state duly opened amidst loud, tumultuous, and long-lasting cheers. Then came the turn of Prime Minister Yonyon of the Cooperative Republic of Yonta. The distinguished apostle of human rights in the region used his speech to paint a graphic portrait of the human rights violations in the region.

"The overflowing tide of human rights abuses in our region has swallowed up the dignity and pride of our people, quenched their latent talents, and reduced them to paupers in a world of abundance. In every station of human sustenance in our hemisphere, people have been stripped naked of their basic inherent rights, making it exceedingly difficult for them to put body and soul together. At the same time, our politicians are swimming in foul-and-evil-smelling wealth and leading prodigal lifestyles.

"We have denied our people their great and imperishable right to free speech, right to assemble, right to vote, and right to worship. We have taken away their sweet and inalienable right to education, right to healthcare, right to work, and right to a fair trial. We have deprived them of their innate and biogenic right to food, clothing, shelter, and safety. Our people are frustrated and angry. Their pent-up frustration and anger could implode anytime, anywhere, and violently blow off all our time-honored institutions and ideologies, throwing us all into a deep sea of anarchy.

"I am talking of a revolution, a revolt by the governed against the governor. As political managers, if we do not change the way we do things in this hemisphere, we will live to regret it. We will become a captive of our own failures and inactions and, perhaps, end up in the walls of the very deplorable prisons, to whose upkeep we have been paying lip service.

"The time is now for us to change, and the change is now for the time. The time is now for us to throw overboard all practices that undermine societal development, and bring onboard practices that drive the forward march of society. The time is now for us to unchain ourselves from practices that have enslaved our women and girls at the shrine of culture and religion. The time is now for us to take the inevitable bold step to embrace democracy and make it the least common denominator in the arithmetic of our affairs. The time is now, and now is the time."

Succinct but weighty. Excellently delivered in a flowing language with a radiogenic voice, and all celebrated the exploit of the Yontanian Prime Minister with a round of thunderous applause. Next came His Excellency Tozaza, the Supreme Religious Leader of Tozan, doubling as the head of state of the country. He began his address, citing a verse from the holy Tozanla scripture, gave a glowing account of the glaring socio-economic inequalities in the region, and appealed for efforts to level the economic playing field in the hemisphere.

"Your Excellencies, nothing could be more gladdening to the heart than once-upon-a-time foes seeking to bury their differences and forge unity. The only time God, ever, feared man was when the entire human race, speaking a common language, came under the umbrella of unity to build a city and a tower tall enough to reach heaven. Had God not confounded their speech so that they could no longer understand one another, humanity would have achieved this far-fetched mission of reaching heaven and, perhaps, uncovering veiled celestial secrets.

"Indeed, there is towering power in unity. Unity commands numbers; unity carries strength; unity showcases variety. However, as we strive to unite our peoples, we should not be dazed by the irresistible dividends of unity to brush aside the chronic inequalities in our societies, that could make unity a virtue not worth practicing.

"Our hemisphere is endowed with abundant natural resources. There is no doubt about that. However, the resources are not equitably distributed. While some of our countries are profusely endowed with resources, some do not have any at all. I am not blaming God for this unfortunate situation. No. God has a reason for everything He does. I am just bringing this anomaly to the attention of your excellencies for it to be factored into the unity formula we are about to devise for the region. Even the so-called ubiquitous resources like water, air, and light which are supposed to be everywhere are no longer anywhere. Economically, the inequality gap between our nations is frightening. The biggest economy in the region has a per capita GDP of US $100,000, while that of the smallest economy is just US $150.

In the area of education, too, there is a yawning inequality gap. While the most refined nation in the region has a literacy rate of nearly 100%, churning out highly qualified professionals and skilled technicians, there are states in the region having literacy rates below 30%, with more than 60% of their labor force tilling the soil with crude implements. How can a tiny insect like the ant forge a doable alliance with a massive mammal like the elephant? Fellow Excellencies, as we take steps to unite our economies and bring hope to our people, we must tread cautiously to avoid creating a monster that will plunge the entire region into bottomless economic chaos."

With that admonition, the Tozanian Supreme Religious Leader, and head of state, ended his speech as he began, reciting a verse from the holy Tozanla scripture. The next to mount the podium, was President Mototo of the Union of

Motolands, the host of the next regional sports festival. As would be expected, he began his address, thanking his colleagues for conferring the honor of hosting the next regional Olympics on his country.

"From the depth of our hearts, we are very grateful for the singular honor of selecting our country to host the second edition of our regional Olympic Games. We know what the games will bring to us as a nation. We are aware of the compelling power of sports to promote peace, understanding, tolerance, and social cohesion among our people. We are also cognizant of the persuading power of sports to define national identity and enhance national unity. We are not oblivious to the overriding value-added role sports play in molding the athlete's overall corporate personality. Sports' inherent values of teamwork, determination, fairness, discipline, respect, and passion for fitness build the character of athletes and help them develop strategic and analytic thinking to acquire rare leadership skills.

"We in the Union of Motolands see sports as an effective tool for building a regional coalition like the one we are on the verge of inaugurating. A sports jamboree, like the one we now own in this region, has the power to dismantle national, social, ethnic, and religious barriers dividing us. And we salute His Highness Emperor Vovovo for originating this annual sports celebration.

"Your Excellencies, we are aware of our status as the smallest nation in the hemisphere. In fact, we know that the size of the largest nation in the region is about 120 times that of ours. However, Lilliputians as we are, we will not allow ourselves to be intimated by any Goliath or

Brobdingnagian in the region. We will flex our muscles and demand what belongs to us. In an assembly of sovereign nations, equity is the only idiom of expression. And we promise to expressly express this idiom by unmistakably performing our obligations and stubbornly demanding and defending our rights.

"We know that every member-state of our soon-to-be-commissioned union, irrespective of the size or population, has only one vote. And we promise to wisely use our solitary vote to take decisions that will help crown our region as the champions of the rule of law, human rights, and democracy in the world. For our tiny size, the Union of Motolands is mockingly referred to as the 'Ant of the Hemisphere.' Yes, we are aware of that, and we are proud of it, knowing that the intelligence of the tiny ant exceedingly surpasses that of the immense elephant. Yes, intelligence is our main resource, and it is an exportable commodity. We are ready to deploy our far-reaching intelligence to the length and breadth of our region to help it attain the ultimate," the head of state of Motolands concluded and exited the podium.

The audience devotedly acknowledged and celebrated the import of President Mototo's brilliant speech with a spontaneous standing ovation. It was now the turn of General Popog of the Communality of Pogan. Beautifully attired in a military uniform, colorfully displaying a horde of military medals, the five-star general, athletically mounted the podium to deliver his address. He began by explaining the reasons behind the frequent dawn broadcasts that had distinguished his country as the most militarily-harassed human habitat on the planet.

"Your Excellencies, Ladies and, Gentlemen, there is no doubt, that the Communality of Pogan has, over the years, acquired notoriety in military take-overs and has deservedly been nicknamed the 'Warehouse of Coups.' Since Pogan gained independence some fifty years ago, it has witnessed thirty successful military coups, making it an average of a coup every twenty months. We have, on record, a soldier scoring a hat-trick in coup-making and another scoring a brace. We even had a nephew overthrowing his uncle and later appointing him as his chief adviser and, worse of all, a son overthrowing his own father. This sad chapter of our history is a big worry to many Poganians, including some of us in uniform.

"It was the desire to end the cycle of military coups in Pogan that prompted me to seize power four years ago. In my take-over address, I described my coup as 'the last of all coups,' and promised to perform the last funeral rites for coups in the country. It is a credit to my coup that Poganian politics has traveled four long years without slipping into the abyss of instability. My fellow men and women in uniform, most often, give hilarious reasons for dismantling the apparatus of the state. One of them accused the civilian politicians of taking all the beautiful ladies in town, leaving the soldiers in romantic distress. Another simply said, 'We, soldiers want to be part of the decision-making process of the country.' Academicians seem to be struggling in vain to accurately explain the reasons behind the recurring military coups in my country.

"Fellow Excellencies, I have not done any research on the subject but I believe it is the political culture of 'the winner takes all' that has created the space for the regular military flirtation in politics in Pogan. Whenever the soldiers seize power, they give a catalogue of corruption-headlined grievous economic and political sins the civilian politicians had committed and promise to drain the swamps breeding corruption. However, in the process of draining the swamps, the coup-makers get stuck in the very swamps they are draining. They commit more grievous sins and are also overthrown by another set of soldiers. And the cycle of political instability goes on and on, gradually turning coup-making into the highest point of attainment in the soldiering profession.

"However, we cannot continue to chart the path of disturbing the peace of the region with an embarrassment of military coups d'état. No, there must be an end, and the end is here, and the end is me. Since mounting the Poganian political stage, I have put together a program dedicated to re-educating and re-training our soldiers to change their mindset from coup-making to focusing on their core mandate of defending the territorial integrity of the country. I have also created a civic education commission, tasked to educate the citizenry on their rights and responsibilities to enable them to become active participants of the political process.

"Your Excellencies, it is my hope that the innovative economic arrangement we are about to unveil will help accelerate the pace of political change in Pogan. No state in this hemisphere needs change more than Pogan. We need change to end the atrocious human rights abuses in our country. We need change to end the looting of the resources of our country. We need change to end the regular military coups in our country. Pogan needs change to give hope to its people."

After the rallying call for change in every spectrum of Poganian life, General Popog resumed his seat while drawing long applause from devotees of change. Now, came the turn of President Wowon of the Homeland of Wongo, the respected law professor, whose professorship and law practice had taken him to all the countries in the region. As an aficionado of democracy, he opened his case for unity in the region by erecting a magnificent architecture for democracy as an effective agent of peace and development.

"Where pure democracy thrives, freedom flowers, peace persists, innovation takes place, progress flourishes, and the horizons of human civilization expand. This time-tested truth holds in all human habitats, under all conditions. However, where contaminated democracy is on duty, freedom stunts, peace goes on trial, innovation stagnates, progress dips and the horizons of human civilization diminish. This is another time-tested truth, and, unfortunately, this is the truth ruling our world here in Sunrise Hemisphere.

"Almost all the varying editions of democracy ever practiced in our region, do not meet the acid-test for true democracy. They are all diverse forms of dictatorship beautifully clothed in the cosmetics of democracy. They lack the ingredients which make democracy total and complete, and worth practicing. The building blocks for true democracy are the effective participation of citizens in politics and civic life, the guarantee of equality and justice for all, the protection of basic human rights, and an effective system for recruiting leadership via free and fair elections.

"Fellow Excellencies, none of these benchmarks of democracy really exist in any of our countries. Our people lack political literacy and cannot adequately contribute to the national political discourse. Our people do not know their basic human rights, let alone demand and claim them. Though equality, freedom, and justice feature prominently on the national emblems of many of our countries, our people have never known the true color of freedom, justice, and equality. Though elections are a quadrennial ritual in most of our countries, election results have never reflected the true will of the people.

"The most rigged election ever recorded on this planet happened in one of our countries. That was in 1927. The winner of the presidential election obtained 243,000 votes at the time the registered voters in the country were less than 15,000. How do we explain this? And how do we also explain the situation of a presidential candidate obtaining no vote at a polling station, where he and his dear wife and four beloved children cast their votes?

"Your Excellencies, these are the dilemmas of our world. And why will we not face these kinds of electoral dilemmas when the umpires for elections are always recruited by the head of state? How impartial will a football referee be when he is appointed by one of the competing sides? Even, in the age of VAR, he can never be wholly neutral. This explains why our electoral politics is elegantly clothed in disputes.

"Fellow Excellencies, permit me to point out this anomaly that is extremely unmaking our nations. We, presidents in this region, are too powerful. It appears we have the power to do anything and everything, anywhere and everywhere in our countries. We, the presidents, appoint the chief justice and the judges of the supreme court. We appoint the head of the elections body. We also appoint the head of the armed forces, the police, the fire service, immigration, customs, prisons, and the national bureau of investigation. That is not all. We, again, appoint the accountant-general and the auditor-general. We, further, appoint ministers of state, heads of parastatals and their boards, as well as heads of local government administrations.

"Every officeholder in our region seems to be at our beck and call. This overriding power to hire and fire reduces us presidents to nothing more than dictators issuing decrees. Unless and until we devise a formula to curtail the powers of our presidents, the bright sun of hope can never appear on our horizon. The reality is that we are running toy governments with rubber-stamp institutions and not democracies."

After calling for the scaling down of the powers of presidents to allow for the operation of true democracy in the region, Wongolese President Wowon left the podium while his inspirational delivery was celebrated with a round of ear-splitting applause. The last to speak was His Highness Emperor Vovovo of the Venomous Empire of Voberia, the convener of the summit. He dedicated his address to the youth, describing them as the unfortunate legatees of the deep ocean of political mess that had swallowed up the region.

"Fellow Excellencies, are we aware that we have a milk of blooming youthful talents in our countries, and that the future of our region depends on harnessing these talents? Unfortunately, our bad governance has forced too many of our young men and women to make cemeteries of their lives by burying their talents. We have failed to create the needed space for our youth to fully utilize their talents. It is said that the real tragedy in life is not the limitation to only one talent but the failure to fully utilize this one talent.

"We have turned our youth into a worried generation. They are disturbed and worried about the decayed economies in their countries, depriving them of jobs. They are upset and worried about the alarming rate at which corruption is contaminating every sector of public life. They are scared and worried about the frightening rate at which immorality is wedding every segment of human civilization. They are terrified and worried about the amazing speed with which their green vegetations are turning gray.

"These are the worries of our young men and women. We have mortgaged their future and turned them into a dispossessed generation on a sinking ship. Disturbed and confused, some of them have sought asylum in impious life, allowing drugs to take them, hostage. Some have condemned themselves to the dictates of other forms of immorality. There are others, who are daring and have become an escape of economic refugees, embarking on dangerous journeys across tempestuous seas, on overcrowded unseaworthy boats in search of comfort abroad. During these journeys, many of them perish through dehydration and shipwrecks.

"Fellow Excellencies, this is the untold story of our youth. Disgusting, pitiful, far-fetching, and heartless. And it is for this reason that we should dedicate our gathering here today to our young men and women, unveiling a comprehensive blueprint to chart a bright future for them. I am convinced that in unity we can do this.

"When we are united, we can be each other's keeper, keeping watch over each other's governance but not rudely interfering. In unity, we will share our resources, jointly exploit them, and collectively enjoy the benefits. In unity, we will share knowledge to eradicate poverty, ignorance, and disease. Swapping resources is the wisest theory in economics; unity will galvanize us to practice this noble principle and have plenty in the midst of want. Sharing is the secret of fellowship because happiness is not complete if it is not shared. We will share everything that has a name, even our pains, frustrations, and sorrows.

"However, for us to accomplish this laudable vision, we have to embrace change, giving away all things that deter progress and taking on new things that sponsor progress. As we ride along the road of change to bring rejuvenation, innovation, opportunity, and progress to our world, we should bear in mind that we will inescapably trip over the potholes of instability, upheaval, unpredictability, threat, and disorientation. We should not be deterred; they are the barriers to the kingdom of change. We should fight on and fight out to overcome them."

With the rallying cry for change, Emperor Vovovo ended his address and received overwhelming approval, expressed in a sincere and vociferous applause from his colleague heads of state and the entire gathering. His speech brought to an end proceedings for Day One of the two-day summit. The lively facial expression, publicized by the heads of state at the end of the deliberations, abundantly showed their satisfaction with what had so far taken place.

Day Two was a closed-door meeting of the heads of state and their economic and foreign affairs ministers. It was a session for painstaking haggling and bargaining among the heads of state. They wanted to incorporate the expectations and fears of each of the nations into the working document that would create the regional union. This was to make the document acceptable to all. The deliberations went on deep into midnight before the heads of state emerged out of the meeting to issue what they called the Zo City Declaration.

The seven-point declaration created the Economic Union of the Sunrise Hemisphere to be headquartered in Mo City, the capital of the Union of Motolands, the tiniest nation in the regional grouping. The declaration also established a seven-member Committee of Eminent Scholars, one from each state, to review all cultural norms and practices detrimental to peace, unity, and development of the region.

The declaration, additionally, created a regional electoral body to be known as the Sunrise Hemisphere Elections Board. The nine-member, all-female body would be responsible for conducting elections in all the seven states of the region. Tired and frustrated with the high-level electoral corruption, election disputes, and heartbreaks associated with men-led election bodies in the region, the leaders opted to try the patience of women. As would be expected, the heads of state nominated Yo City, the capital of Yonta, the most entrenched democracy in the region, to house the headquarters of the regional elections body. Dates were set for the inauguration of the newly created regional institutions.

Zolandese King Zozozo addressed the closing session, urging his fellow heads of state to fully implement all the decisions taken at the summit to ensure a smooth take-off of the newly created regional institutions. He warned that failure to do so would spell doom for the region, and exacerbate the sufferings of the people. The heads of state patted themselves on the back for the historic summit, while the media hailed their achievement as a monumental development that could turn the fortunes of the region.

Chapter Ten
The New-Look
Sunrise Hemisphere

Three weeks after the summit, all the regional institutions were inaugurated at elaborate ceremonies and became fully operational. Piecemeal implementation of the protocols of the economic union began with the free movement of people, goods, and services across national borders. This culminated in the availability of a wide range of goods and services in every country in the region, giving the people a variety to choose from, intensifying competition and bringing down prices. This development endeared the hearts of the people, who applauded their leaders for putting together such a wonderful arrangement to improve their conditions of living.

While all this was happening, Princess Vovona had intensified her romantic overtures toward me. She had increased the frequency of her visits and even invited me to spend a weekend with her at her father's imposing palace in Vo City, a request I was not able to honor. She had also increased the rate at which she was greedily flooding me with all manners of presents, even gifting me an expensive car. At this juncture, the princess seemed to have traveled on a journey from nowhere to somewhere, attempting to open the air-tight lid firmly covering our secret love.

Indeed, rumors began flying across national frontiers, around the region, about a hidden plan of the revered Voberian emperor to give out his princess to tie the knot with a young man from Zoland. However, such rumors were swiftly dispatched into the dustbin of gossip mongering, as interstate marriage was a grievous cultural sin punishable by banishment in the region. Moreover, many people thought it would be outrageous and irrational on the part of the venerable emperor to give out his only daughter, and heiress-apparent, for marriage outside the confines of his territory. Nonetheless, the rumor persisted, gaining currency in Zoland, with the sensational *Zo City Herald* tabloid reporting extensively on it.

With the thundering headline, '*A Zolandese Becomes Emperor in Voberia,*' the paper alleged that giving out the princess for marriage in Zoland was one of the several bargaining chips the Voberian emperor put on offer to seal his regional economic union proposition. The paper disclosed that the planned royal marriage had the blessing of the Zolandese monarch. However, the paper could not name the lucky Zolandese beneficiary of the deal.

At the same time, the Committee of Eminent Scholars tasked to review cultural practices undercutting development in the region had concluded its work and had submitted its report to the regional leaders. Topping the list of nine cultural practices identified to be extremely inimical to societal unity and development in the region was the taboo on interstate marriage. The regional heads of state voted overwhelmingly to accept the report and accordingly agreed to expunge the nine pieces of traditional legislation from the cultural code of the region. There was, however, one dissenting vote, Tozanian Supreme Religious Leader, Tozaza voted against the annulment, arguing that it would promote a wholesale importation of foreign cultures into the various countries in the region and fatally bleach the identity of the people.

The decision to annul the perceived retrogressive cultural decrees, especially the taboo on interstate marriage, received mixed reactions across the length and breadth of the region. Broad-minded citizens welcomed it as a long-awaited opportunity to purge the region of the residues of barbarism and anarchism to pave the way for the forward march of the region. However, ultra-conservatives and political hawks saw it as an abominable act that would offend the gods and bring untold curses to the region.

Throughout the hemisphere, the annulment of the taboos had become a hot-button talking point, deafeningly justified at the corridors of scholarship and modernity and mutely whispered and condemned at the shrines of tradition and conservatism. A coalition against the cancellation of the taboos began growing in all states and ultimately developed into an effective regional movement sponsored by wealthy ultra-conservatives. The "No to Change Movement," as they called themselves, had been beaming their messages to powerful traditionalists, religious organizations, and the aged.

On the other hand, the reformists, who had coalesced into the "Yes for Progress Movement," drew their support largely from the intelligentsia. They had been targeting the youth, schools, universities, and churches with their human-rights-headlined messages. The thrilling debate, which received intensive media coverage, appeared to have dismantled national boundaries and virtually turned the entire Sunrise Hemisphere region into two distinct ideological geographies: the "No to Change Movement," and the "Yes for Progress Movement." It became a fierce, borderless, ideological contest between the Yeas and the Nays.

Interesting development indeed! The once-upon-a-time national patriots, who were submissively saluting national flags and proudly singing national anthems of their respective countries, had now forgotten their national pride and identity and were now forming unlikely alliances under the banner of ideology. A few political heavyweights in the region openly declared their ideological stance. Tozanian Supreme Religious Leader Tozaza threw his weight behind the "No to Change Movement," while democracy-enthused Yontanian Prime Minister Yonyon identified himself with the "Yes for Progress Movement."

As the ferocious debate persevered, political heads in the region met and decided to hold a referendum to put the matter to rest. This was to be the first assignment for the newly created regional elections body, the Sunrise Hemisphere Elections Board. A carefully strategized electioneering process got underway, with the two sides deploying well-oiled campaign machinery similar to those put up by political parties. They employed the services of campaign managers and political activists known as foot soldiers, who put in motion a wide range of fundraising activities, including donations from individuals and corporate entities.

Ironically, the two sides brought into play similar campaign strategies, utilizing retail and wholesale campaign techniques: holding big rallies and engaging in door-to-door canvassing. They further, made extensive use of commercial advertising and a mixture of public relations and entertainment known as *politainment*. Both sides also had, at their disposal, an array of branded promotional items such as T-shirts, hats, bumper stickers, stress balls, banners, balloons, keyholders, pens, notebooks, and scarfs, which they generously gave out to supporters and sympathizers.

After four weeks of an acrimonious campaign, marked by violence, bickering, and name-calling, the well-resourced Sunrise Hemisphere Elections Board conducted the referendum, and within twenty-four hours, the results were out. The "Yes for Progress Movement" had a landslide victory, winning in all seven states and obtaining more than 74% percent of the votes. It was a resounding victory, joyously celebrated by supporters and sympathizers of the "Yes for Progress Movement" throughout the region.

While the Yeas were celebrating their unquestionable victory, the political leadership of the region were also celebrating the unquestionable manner the newly created regional elections body had conducted the referendum. At a special ceremony, attended by all regional leaders, special awards were presented to the nine-member all-female regional electoral body for conducting a free, fair, and transparent poll. The regional leaders also hailed the timely release of the referendum results, noting that while it could take weeks to months to release election results in the region, the regional electoral body took just twenty-four hours to do so. This, the regional leaders pointed out, nipped in the bud anxieties, and tensions associated with delayed election results declarations.

As for the disappointed vanquished Nays, though they did not dispute the referendum results, they largely blamed the media for their poor performance. They accused the media of not providing them with the needed platform to comprehensively articulate their viewpoints. They also accused foreign rightist groups, operating under the disguise of relief agencies, of rudely interfering in the referendum by secretly funding the Yeas. Despite the humiliating defeat, the Nays pledged not to retreat but to continue the fight to preserve the sanctity, pride, and dignity of the region.

The lifting of the ban on interstate marriage saw a sudden boom in weddings across the region, creating a thriving industry of firms producing bridal products and managing nuptial events. Everywhere in the region, wedding ceremonies were taking place. However, the Homeland of Wongo was the preferred destination for most of the men. Wongo has the most beautiful ladies in the region, and every man with a taste for beauty went there. And they came in droves, hungrily and mercilessly poaching all the beauty queens and goddesses in town, to the displeasure of the Wongolese men. Wongo is the only country in the region where women outnumber men by the ratio of six to four, with women often proposing to men for marriage. Despite the supply of women far outstripping the demand, resulting in a large number of unattached women in town, the ferocious raid on Wongolese women from outside became so out-of-control that Wongolese authorities threatened to pull out of the regional union. It took the intervention of heads of state of the region to curb the high waves of the unyielding mass influx of unmarried men into Wongo.

At the same time, there was an unprecedented scramble for Motolandese men. Motolandese men have the highest IQ in the region and are perceived to be the most intelligent people in the region. For this reason, most parents in the region took advantage of the lifting of the ban on interstate marriage to force their daughters to marry Motolandese men in order to introduce the Motolandese gene into their families. In fact, Motolandese men virtually became an endangered species, hounded down and poached by women from all over the hemisphere. The women were openly proposing to them for marriage, offering huge sums of money, expensive cars, posh houses, and unimaginable promises. This development did not go down well with Motolandese women, who had been protesting against what they perceived as the kidnapping of their men by professional prostitutes in the region.

While the predatory gaze of the entire region was on Wongolese women and Motolandese men, news began filtering in of another interesting bridal development in the region. Major news outlets in the region were reporting that His Highness Emperor Vovovo of the Venomous Empire of Voberia had given out his only daughter, Crown Princess Vovona, for marriage in Zoland and that the wedding of the century would very soon be celebrated throughout the region. The media reports did not name the Zolandese husband-to-be. However, historians predicted that tradition heavily favors the King's handsome son, Crown Prince Zozoto, to be the bachelor in contention, as interstate royal marriage was a practice celebrated in the region some six centuries ago.

As the speculations gained currency, King Zozozo began overhauling the political profile of his son in anticipation of the eventuality. The prince, who had been on the fringes of mainstream Zolandese politics, was now headlining key state ceremonies, commissioning projects, receiving emissaries, giving speeches at key state functions, and making huge charitable donations.

The crown prince also began embroiling himself in regional diplomacy, shuttling between national capitals to perform functions on behalf of his father. One of such visits took him to Vo City, the Voberian foremost city, where he had the rare opportunity to hold discussions with Princess Vovona. However, the talks were confined to bilateral relations between the two countries and never strayed into the territory of affection. Though Prince Zozoto extended an invitation to Princess Vovona to visit Zoland, the invitation was never honored.

And finally, the jaw-dropper came. From his sacred palace in Vo City, Emperor Vovovo made the shattering announcement of the imminent marriage of her daughter, Princess Vovona to a little-known Zolandese man. In a terse press statement, which did not disclose the name of the lucky Zolandese would-be husband, the king said the move was to kindle interstate marriage at all levels of society in the region. The surprising announcement reverberated with excitement and confusion across the region, sending media men and women on an adventurous expedition to find out the lucky beneficiary of the emperor's goodwill.

Using the widely published photos that Emperor Vovovo and his daughter took with the Zale family during a visit to Zoland as a lead, a scoop of journalists invaded our house. Investigative reporters, celebrity journalists, political journalists, camera men and women, and a flash of paparazzies were there in their manifold forms and numbers. And we were all terrified. Surprisingly, secret police from King Zozozo's palace were also there. Poor Zifi, as well, had her father's house invaded by journalists as she too appeared in the much-celebrated photos the Zale family took with the Voberian emperor and his princess.

The situation became so tense and worrying that I was smuggled out of Vo City to the village to live with my parents. However, it did not take long for the secret police to begin coming there too. And they were coming with increasing regularity, interrogating us on all manner of issues. It was a terrifying moment for us. We were virtually under house arrest. They policed all our movements, even on the farm. However, this could not stop my regular phone calls with Princess Vovona. I gave her every detail of the hell of policing my parents and I were going through in the village. I also told her about the sad state of affairs in Uncle Zale's house, with the house practically put under siege by grilling secret police officers and a contingent of probing journalists.

As things were getting out of hand, with my life practically under threat, I was smuggled out of the village to the Voberian Embassy in Zo City. The embassy became my new home. I was doing everything there, from dusk to dawn, living a relatively comfortable life. I was taking good meals, and given first-class facilities for recreation. I was also provided a hit-tec gym for daily work-outs. I had at my disposal, all I needed to be well informed about happenings in the region. There were radio and television sets, as well as the latest copies of major newspapers and magazines in the region. Furthermore, I continued receiving regular phone calls from Princess Vovona. No Zolandese knew my whereabouts, except Sister Zizi and Uncle Zale, who occasionally visited me.

After staying in the embassy for more than three months, I was, one day, driven out of the embassy at dawn to the airport and hastily thrown into a plane. And, finally, I found myself in Yo City, the Yontanian capital. To my surprise, Princess Vovona was at the airport to receive me. It was a joyful moment for me to see her. She hugged me and gave me a stimulating kiss. From the airport, we were driven to a posh house near the Voberian embassy in Yonta, which was to be my next home for months to come. Another surprise was awaiting me here, too. And it came in the surprised emergence from the house of the old brigade of four—Uncle Zale, Sister Zizi, Little Zito, and Zifi—to welcome me.

It was an unexpected reunion, and we highly cherished it and excessively celebrated it. Indeed, it was the mystery girl who pulled up a few of the numerous mysteries up her sleeve to rescue us in our trying moments. She masterminded my escape from the village to the Voberian embassy in Zo City and finally to Yo City. She was also the mastermind of the fleeing of the Zale family from Zo City to Yo City. Since the day I arrived, the Yontanian authorities began providing us 24-hour security and offering us other courtesies as if we were diplomats.

As all this was happening, a wildfire of confusion was devouring the Venomous Empire of Voberia, tearing it apart. A movement of resistance against the proposed marriage of Princess Vovona to a Zolandese had sprung up, occasioning daily mass demonstrations in major cities and towns across the country. The epicenter of the resistance, Vota City—the cultural capital of the country—had vowed to do everything possible, if even pulling down the heavens, to stop the marriage. The Votaians argued that such a marriage would gravely bleach the authenticity of the Voberian culture and effortlessly transfer the kingship of the empire to Zoland, their archenemy.

At this point, it was no longer a secret that I was the Zolandese young man within an ace of marrying the Voberian heiress-apparent. The imminent royal marriage had been reported widely in the media, with my pictures splashed on the front pages of major newspapers and magazines throughout the region. The media went further, compiling a profile on me and digging into the background of my parents. One newspaper even reported that my parents were not native Zolandese and that their grandparents migrated from elsewhere to settle there.

The newspaper report, doubting the Zolandese nationality of my parents, prompted the Sociology Department of the University of Vo City to carry out in-depth research on the genealogy of my family. After thorough research, it emerged that, indeed, my parents were not native Zolandese, and that their grandparents were Voberians who migrated to Zoland some two-and-a-half centuries ago during a bloody inter-clan fighting that accounted for the loss of thousands of lives and the burning down of several towns and villages.

It also emerged that my great grandparents came from the royal Vota clan. It was further discovered that, until the bloody inter-clan fighting leading to the emigration of my great grandparents, the rulership of Voberia was alternating between the Vota clan of my great grandparents and the Vovo clan of Princess Vovona's great grandparents. It was the relocation of my great-grandparents to Zoland that handed over the Voberian rulership monopoly to the Vovo clan. The findings concluded that Vota City, the epicenter of the resistance against the marriage, was, in fact, the birthplace of my great grandparents. A DNA test confirmed that I was undeniably a royal of the Vota clan of Voberia. The university's findings were widely publicized throughout the region.

The new development compelled the Votaians to eat humble pie and abandon their affirmed project of stopping the marriage. Instead, they made a sharp U-turn and began mobilizing efforts to root for the proposed wedlock, calling it a marriage between two royals. Nationwide, the demonstrations ceased and sanity returned to the country. Elsewhere in the region, tensions bordering on the marriage eased. The hierarchy of Zolandese leadership had now accepted the reality of the mercurial transformation of an ordinary Zolandese into a Voberian royal, on line to pair up with another Voberian royal and, undeniably, an heiress-apparent. The public knowledge of the two personalities involved in the looming royal marriage did not, however, end the whispers in the Sunrise Hemisphere. The whispers continued, conjecturing the nature, form, and character of the marriage and how it would affect the dynamics of politics in the entire region.

Now excited about the possibility of the rulership of Voberia coming back to them again, the Vota clan invited me to a special ceremony in Vota City at which a befitting Voberian name would be conferred on me. On the day of the ceremony, my parents together with the four old brigade—Uncle Zale, Sister Zizi, Little Zito, and Zifi—came down to support me. Of course, Princess Vovona was abundantly there too. The political and traditional hierarchy of the powerful Vota clan, including provincial and local administrators as well as traditional and religious heads, were all there in their numbers to grace the occasion.

During, what was described as an initiation ceremony, a series of rites—each marked by the firing of a musket—were performed, after which a fat bull was slaughtered. I was then ushered into a sacred room where I was robed in a Votaian traditional war dress and given a special sword. With the sword in my right hand, I was rushed back to the ceremony ground and spontaneously greeted with shouts of "Emperor Vototo, Emperor Vototo, Emperor Vototo." An oldster then got hold of my hand, introduced me to the gathering as Prince Vototo, and declared that I was no longer to be known and called Zaza. He went on to explain that I was named after my great-great-great-great-great-great grandfather, the powerful 16th century Voberian Emperor Vototo, who conquered and colonized all Sunrise Hemisphere states and even made incursions into a few states in the Sunset Hemisphere.

While the ceremony was at its climax, I spotted Princess Vovona casting a graceful look at me and smiling. The brief ceremony had extensive media coverage and took a front-page headline in most of the major newspapers in the region. The entire ceremony was carried live on radio and television in all seven states of the region.

Chapter Eleven
The Wedding of the Century

The date for the royal wedding, branded the "Wedding of the Century," was now known and preparations were earnestly underway. In the Sunrise Hemisphere, weddings are a communal festival fully funded by voluntary contributions from members of the community. The groom and bride do not spend anything, not even a dime, so do their families too; they don't spend anything. As a community event, weddings are enthusiastically celebrated by the entire community, and the celebrations could last up to four weeks. In light of this, the seven countries in the region were deeply involved in the planning of every aspect of the royal wedding and were each assigned roles to play. The roles were carefully given according to the competence and comparative advantage of each of the countries. The countries were told to do their level best to excel in their assigned tasks to collectively make the wedding a resounding success and memorable.

As the leading producer of the most beautiful girls in the region, the Homeland of Wongo was given the responsibility of providing the bride maids. They were told to assemble the hundred most mouth-wateringly alluring beauties the world-outside-Wongo had never seen before. The cast was to be made up of crème de la crème of the latest editions of known beauty, inclusive of dreamy beauty, heavenly beauty, drop-dead beauty, sublime beauty, and heart-stopping beauty. In the line-up was also to be ravishing beauty, riveting beauty, seductive beauty, smoking hot beauty, winsome beauty, and other subsets of stunning beauty. However, all the girls must be Immaculate Marys, sinlessly stainless. A virginity test should be conducted to ensure their stainlessness.

Having distinguished itself as the gastronomical capital of the region, very adept in the art and science of good cooking and good eating, the Cooperative Republic of Yonta was tasked to prepare food to feed all the guests at the wedding. They were charged to bring together their renowned chefs to prepare yummy, flavorful lip-smacking dishes that would reflect the gastronomic diversity of the region. The Yontanians were told to prepare tons of food to satiate the yearnings of all present and, as well, deploy smartly dressed courteous tray trotters to serve.

The responsibility for providing drinks at the wedding fell on the Communality of Pogan, a kleptocratic state, notoriously famous for consistently operating kakistocracy and khakistocracy, with military officers, time and again, taking over the commanding heights of national politics. The leaders have distinguished themselves in thievery and bad governance but exceedingly excelling in leading prodigal lifestyles, copiously consuming very expensive wines and gins. The Poganians were tasked to make good use of their top-class wine brewers and wine testers as well as their best gin makers to assemble the highest-known quality of wines and gins in the world. They were also told to make available exceptionally high-quality diamond-coated wine glasses for serving very important dignitaries.

The Indomitable Kingdom of Zoland took charge of providing entertainment at the wedding. Having distinguished itself as the Las Vegas of the region, where sentimental dreams come true, Zoland was to dig deep into its array of rich entertainment talents and put together a series of extraordinary shows at every intersection of an event during the month-long celebrations. Zoland appeared to be apt to this task. It had for more than a century been holding annual entertainment events like cultural festivals, musical concerts, dancing contests, award shows, beauty pageants, and cooking contests and has virtually become the tourism hub of the region. Zoland was directed to recruit highly professional dancers from its performing arts institutions, especially that of the University of Zo City to put on show evocative, gravity-defying, interpretive body movement and facial expression dances denoting all the best wishes newlyweds need for honeymooning.

In addition to being in charge of entertainment, Zoland was also to provide an expressive personality with a sense of humor to emcee the grand reception to climax the month-long wedding celebrations. Without any consultations, His Majesty King Zozozo unilaterally elected his son, Crown Prince Zozoto, to carry out this celebrity kind of assignment. And the eloquent handsome prince with a dazzling personality and magnificent stage presence appeared to have the mojo to hold the audience spellbound and warmly interact with them. Paradoxically, when the ban on interstate marriage was lifted, the Zolandese heir-apparent conceived the idea of marrying the Voberian heiress-apparent and tirelessly worked toward it in vain.

For the task of providing voguish dresses with matching accessories for the bride and groom, as well as their attendants, the Union of Motolands was the overwhelming choice. The tiny nation had, over the years, established itself as the preferred fashion destination in the region. It has the men and women capable of manufacturing glorious, fashionable dresses adorned with decorative fittings. Motolands was given the duty of assembling top couturiers to make very expensive handcrafted dresses for the bride and her maids as well as the groom and his men. The dresses, to be made of clothes of luxurious fabrics, should impeccably fit the bride and groom as well as the 'I do crew.' Additionally, the Motolandese were strictly directed to ensure that the wedding gown was accessorized with a diamond tiara.

The brief given to the Motolandese specifically charged them to robe the bride and groom in a unique mode to make them appear matchlessly dazzling, gracefully elegant, glitteringly glamourous, amazingly jaw-dropping, and outstandingly stunning. Not only that. They were to equally appear charmingly magnetic, bewitchingly mesmerizing, engagingly enchanting, flamboyantly exuberant, and spiritedly vivacious. A herculean task indeed, but the crafty Motolandese seemed to be up to it.

The Commonwealth of Tozan, the only theocratic state in the economic union, was put in charge of the décor. The religion-intoxicated country was tasked to deck out the entire wedding ground and the reception hall in rare romantic flowers, giving the reception hall an outlook of a tropical rainforest. The Tozanians were explicitly directed to use specific flowers in the décor.

Purple lilac was to be used to represent the beginning of love; sunflower, to denote longevity, adoration, and pure love; and red camellias, to illustrate 'you are a flame in my heart'. The primrose flower was to be included to carry the message, 'our love is eternity'; while the highly scented stock flower, representing bonds of affection, was to convey the message, 'you will always be beautiful to me.' The forget-me-not flower was to feature prominently to denote love and romance, while the presence of the daisy flower in the line-up was to symbolize innocence and purity. In all, Tozan needed $500,000 worth of rare romantic flowers to adequately accomplish this task. However, being the leading producer and exporter of flowers in the region, word of mouth from its autocratic Supreme Religious Leader would see this assignment fully accomplished within a blink of an eye.

The hosts, the Venomous Empire of Voberia, were assigned a mixed bag of duties to perform. They were to provide the wedding cake, security, groomsmen, and fireworks. They were directed to assemble hundreds of their renowned bakers and chefs to prepare a cake that stretches seven meters to symbolize the seven states in the region. The three-tier cake was to be decorated with 10,000 diamonds. The hosts were further tasked to make available 1,500 kilograms of fireworks to be displayed to bid goodbye to the epic evening of the wedding. The fireworks were estimated to cost $700,000. Regarding the groomsmen, Voberia was advised to recruit all of them from the groom's ancestry Vota clan. For security, Voberia was told to deploy a contingent of 10,000 police and military personnel.

Now, all the states appeared to have adequately rehearsed their roles and were hot-ready for the "Wedding of the Century." Wongo had assembled its rare and incogitable beauty empresses that could invoke the envy of every enquiring eye. Yonta had in its possession a yummy menu of fiery, savory, and crispy courses of nectarous and toothsome dishes that would induce salivation in every human species. Motolands had delicately and intricately made all the wedding dresses and was poised to launch a fashion revolution that would shake the very foundations of human enlightenment. As for Tozan, it finished its preparations long before it was even given the assignment, and was ready to miraculously change the ambiance of the entire wedding ground with well-perfumed romance-sponsored colors.

In the case of Zoland, it had concluded all the rehearsals and was only waiting for the green light to let go the roaring melodic sounds, accompanied by the graceful, fluid, supple, and balletic body movements supplemented with enigmatic facial expressions. Pogan was ready with all manner of drinks—from stiff, strong, and exotic, through wakeful and civil, to refreshingly soft, and deliciously refreshing, together with their accompanying trademark glasses. Voberia, the hosts, had completed baking the seven-meter-long wedding cake and were dying to proudly unveil it as the seventh wonder of the Sunset Hemisphere.

With the lineup for the 'Wedding of the Century' complete, the month-long nuptial celebrations began in earnest, kicking off with pre-wedding activities. The pre-bridal program was so arranged that each of the capitals of the seven countries in the region had the privilege of hosting an event. During each of such events, highly patronized by 'Prince-Weds-Princess'-T-shirts-robed young men and women, there was a glut of merrymaking. Plenty to eat, plenty to drink, plenty to dance, plenty to cheer; a real lovefest, always climaxed by a brief appearance of Princess Vovona and me. And our presence was at all times acknowledged by a jamboree of fanfare and cheers, with all struggling to catch a glimpse of us. In turn, the states delightfully celebrated the pre-wedding events daily, observing it as a public holiday.

The pre-wedding activities went on and on and on and finally arrived the wedding day; bright and sunny. Everything was in apple-pier order. The entire wedding ground was beautifully decked out. Eye-pleasing sentimental colors were cheerfully on parade. Red, blue, pink, gold, and ivory. They were all there and were aromatically perfumed. The political titans of the region, the overlords of the seven states that amazingly sum up the wonderful Sunrise Hemisphere, were all there to spice up the occasion with their majestic presence. A few political heavyweights from the Sunset Hemisphere were also there. And the whole atmosphere was humanly electrifying and angelically Christmassy.

Divinely dressed to the nines, courtesy of the celebrated Motolandese professional couturiers and in the company of glorious friends of honor, we were ushered into the wedding hall by a troupe of singing and dancing Zolandese cultural performers. And quietly, I sat down, with my groomsmen sitting behind me. All eyes were on me, and all my eyes were on all. I spotted my parents and the old brigade of four, occupying prominent seats. They were in a celebratory mood and appeared to have sold all their attention to me, clinically exploring the hand-loomed glad rags enrobing me. And the bright and cheerful countenance they wore, more than assured me of the spick-and-span air I was advertising to the world, and that, indeed, I was dressed to the teeth.

Then, the shouts and the cheers began resonating and were cross-faded into a fanfare. The age-old Zolandese processional wedding song, "The bride is in our midst," immediately followed. And majestically walking her down the aisle, in the company of a hoard of out-of-stock juicy beauty goddesses, was the venerable Emperor Vovovo himself. The bright erotic sun, all were expecting to appear on the horizon of the human eye, had certainly begun dawning. And all were up on their feet, putting on guard their prying eyes to arrest everyone and everything that could arouse human curiosity. And the dignified wedding guests *hosannaed* her as she and her 'I do' crew superbly made their way to their seats. The stately bride, shining bright like a diamond, was now seated, and the "Wedding of the Century" was on, emitting scintillating rays of jollification to homes and hearts of all in the Sunrise Hemisphere and even beyond.

The series of elaborate, awesome rituals that conspire to constitute holy matrimony came and went, until the crescendo, the exchange of vows. And when this important stage of vocalizing words of commitment to seal the marriage was about to commence, a current of uneasiness ran through my body. Fear began taking hold of me and gradually diminishing my confidence level. I hurriedly summoned up a seven-day fasting and prayer deliverance I went through with a prayer warrior friend some time ago and invited the holy spirit to rescue me. The rescue came; the fear fled away; and I pronounced my vow as confidently as a bird committing itself to the air. So did Princess Vovona; she recited her vow as confidently as a great fish committing itself to the ocean deep.

We won the admiration of the audience with our colorful rendition of the vows, and they celebrated our exploits with a deafening standing ovation. The time for the exchange of rings then came. That too went on well, and so were the others that followed. And in a rain of cheers of jubilation, we were unveiled to the gathering as the newest married couple in the universe.

A lip-smacking wedding reception followed. However, before that, a brief colorful ceremony was held to cut the seven-meter-long bridecake. The miracle cake, carrying the emblems of each of the states in the hemisphere, was jointly cut by the seven heads of state of the region. Three heads of state from neighboring Sunset Hemisphere, who attended the wedding, assisted in the cake-cutting sacrament.

The wedding reception itself was more than a funfest staged in a dreamland. The entire reception hall was wonderfully decked out in aromatically-perfumed quixotic colors, creating an awe-inspiring tropical rainforest environment. And here became the abode of anything and everything that generated festivity. Dishes of diverse tastes and textures were there: dry versus crispy, greasy versus velvety, sugary versus honeyed, burned versus blackened, tough versus hearty, mushy versus tender. All the delicious dishes capable of stamping a once-a-life-time memory on an important occasion like a royal wedding, secured prominent positions on the menu. As for the drinks, they were in varying flavors and strengths: from icon rums and cognacs costing as high as $50,000 per bottle, through quality wines costing $1,000 per bottle, to all types of beverages and soft drinks. In attendance was the Zolandese Symphony Orchestra, churning out sweet-flowing fluid tunes to jazz up the celebration. It was a tailor-made party of incalculable worth, sublime and solid-gold, which ended with the displaying of 1,500 kilograms of fireworks, setting the Vo City night skies aglow.

"The 'Wedding of the Century' is officially over, and I am now enrobed in the trappings of a husband and a prince," I kept telling myself, while recalling the zigzagging journey with an unknown destination, which took off from the Zo City Market and eventually ended up in a royal wedding in Vo City. "Ours is a match made in heaven," I concluded, as I wondered how the entire script was perfectly written, and the cast perfectly propelled the gripping narrative to its apogee to make the mystery girl and me an ideal match.

"I am no longer the old, timid, and fear-tyrannized Zaza, always looking for cover at the sight of everything and nothing," I refreshed my memory and tasked myself to unlearn all progress-vitiating traditional values and beliefs and take up the indomitable spirit of my birthplace and the venomous lifeforce of my forebears. "The combination of the two," I noted, "will make me deadly and unconquerable to face the arduous challenges ahead of me in my new role as a prince," I reassured myself.

Doubling now as Prince of Vota Clan and Prince Consort of Voberia, I could not decide on which one of the two labels to wear as my official designation. While Emperor Vovovo and his daughter wanted me to be addressed as Prince Consort of Voberia, the ultra-conservatives and political hawks in Vota Province insisted I should be designated Prince of Vota. A compromise was, however, struck to just call me Prince Vototo. The next dilemma was my official residence: should it be the now-refurbished ancient Vototo Palace in Vota City or the splendid Emperor Vovovo Palace in Vo City? Here too a compromise was reached for me to shuttle between the two palaces.

The final dilemma was my job description, my official duty as a prince in the revered Voberian palace. This hole was very easy to fill, as our royal wedding acted as a magnet pulling together all the states in the region to collectively plan a project, conjointly execute it, and cooperatively inaugurate it. Unsurprisingly, I was assigned the duty of advising the emperor on matters bordering on the unity of states in the Sunrise Hemisphere, and my job title was 'Senior Advisor to the Emperor on Sunrise Hemisphere Unity.'

The oneness with which all the states celebrated the royal wedding took the comradeship in the hemisphere to a higher level, practically dimming the tensions and rancor once ingrained in the DNA of the region. Physical and psychological barriers separating nations began falling apart, creating one huge market for the convergence of sellers and buyers. Certainly, the regional economic union was in full motion, accelerating in top gear. Interstate trade within the region was booming. Regional entities set up to mass-produce common goods and services for the people were producing at full capacity. Social interaction among people from different states was on the increase. Here and there, interstate marriages were taking place on an unparalleled scale. Everywhere in the region, unity was reigning. In truth, the unprecedented unity at work in the region could mobilize resources and energies to build a Towel of Babel to spy on the abode of God and His angels.

The unprecedented unity in the region carried along with it unprecedented peace and progress to the region. And the signs were there for all to see. Everywhere in the region, there was an overabundance of everything; superabundance of food to eat; oversupply of goods and services to satiate human greed; overproduction of variety to match all egos, overflow of festivity to quench all social gratifications. Everywhere in the region, all able-bodied men and women were at work and were excited, expressing their unity-sponsored contentment with whispers of joy and murmurs of love. But, for how long would the unity be sustained to keep the people whispering their joy and murmuring their love?